D1092225

Love
is
Love

Love is Love

METTE BACH

JAMES LORIMER & COMPANY LTD., PUBLISHERS
TORONTO

James Lorimer & Company Ltd., Publishers acknowledges the support of
the Ontario Arts Council (OAC), an agency of the Government of Ontario,
which in 2015-16 funded 1,676 individual artists and 1,125 organizations in
209 communities across Ontario for a total of $50.5 million. We acknowledge
the support of the Canada Council for the Arts, which last year invested $153
million to bring the arts to Canadians throughout the country. This project has
been made possible in part by the Government of Canada and with the support of the Ontario Media Development Corporation.

Cover design: Tyler Cleroux
Cover image:Shutterstock

978-1-4594-1232-3
eBook also available 978-1-4594-1210-1

Cataloguing data available from Library and Archives Canada.

Published by:
James Lorimer & Company Ltd.,
Publishers
117 Peter Street, Suite 304
Toronto, ON, Canada
M5V 0M3
www.lorimer.ca

Distributed by:
Lerner Publisher Services
1251 Washington Ave N
Minneapolis, MN, USA
55401
www.lernerbooks.com

Printed and bound in Canada.
Manufactured by Friesens Corporation in Altona, Manitoba, Canada in
January 2017.
Job #229628

01 Someone Like You

IT WAS 4:24 IN THE MORNING. Emmy sat down in a stairwell just off Osborne. There was some cardboard there, left by someone else. Ty seemed happy enough with that. Emmy felt the relief in her feet first, the warmth that gathered there after a whole night of walking. Ty put his arm around her, pulled her in close, and kissed the back of her head. It was a dream, this night. Being here with Ty.

Ty Biggs was not someone Emmy would normally

talk to. She wouldn't even dream of hanging out with him. But now here she was — his maybe-girlfriend. Ty didn't commit. Everyone knew that. But did he kiss the back of every girl's head?

She looked out at the street. Winnipeg's Osborne Village looked different at this hour. The streetlights looked like squished together moons held up on podiums.

Emmy's stomach rumbled and she hoped Ty hadn't heard it. But he must have, because he reached into his backpack and pulled out a half-eaten hoagie from earlier that night. In the bright lights of the 7-Eleven, Emmy had opted for just an apple. Big mistake. She knew it would never last her through the night, but she couldn't eat in front of Ty. There was no way she could force anything down. Even sitting on the stairs, ravenous and cold, she almost said no to his offer. But he peeled back the plastic wrap and took a big bite, then passed it to her. The smell of ham and yellow mustard was too much to resist. She took a small bite and chewed slowly.

LOVE IS LOVE

"So what now?" she asked when the sandwich was done.

He shrugged. "Not sure. You sleepy?"

"Me? No. Not after all that coffee we drank."

"That stuff doesn't affect me."

"That's cool." Emmy held on to Ty's arm as he reached around her. She patted his forearm like they were an old married couple. Was that cool? She tried to pretend that she had done this sort of thing before.

She reached into her purse and took out her notebook, handling it gently, like a precious jewel. It was the first time she considered opening it for anyone and she had gone over the scene so many times. In her fantasy, she was always at the swingset in the park. Ty was pushing her gently back and forth as he asked to see it.

"Sometimes I write poems," Emmy said now, the book in her hand. She had dog-eared the page she wanted to show Ty, the lines she felt best revealed her. "Would you like me to read you one?"

Ty looked puzzled. "Maybe after. Er, later."

He took her face in his hands and cupped it between his palms. Emmy felt like a chipmunk with his hands enfolding the roundness of her rosy cheeks.

Ty kissed her. Then he unzipped his baggy jeans and offered himself. He didn't have to say a word. She knew what he wanted. As she bent over, she thought about the elite group she was joining. All the girls who had blown Ty had moved up several rungs on the school social ladder.

Emmy hoped it was safe, that he wouldn't give her HPV like in those awful pamphlets at the school nurse's office. But what was the worst that could happen? Would a visit to the doctor be any more shameful than showing her face at school week after week with no stories to tell, no one talking about her? Emmy had nothing worth noting about her except for her dead dad, last year's fashion, and her muffin top. And no one cared about any of that stuff.

Ty leaned back and guided her face downward. She opened her mouth and did what she figured she was supposed to do. Was he into it? She couldn't tell.

LOVE IS LOVE

She wanted him to be. She wanted some hint that she was doing it right. She wanted to hear moaning, but he didn't make a sound. Even a thumbs up would have been better than the torment of his silence.

Emmy's neck was sore when Ty pushed her away. He took over himself, his eyes focused on the wall behind her. Finally, there was a quiet grunt followed quickly by the zip of his jeans.

He didn't ask to hear a poem. Emmy watched the darkness fade. She listened to the first sounds of the morning. She heard the cars of people going to work, living their sad little lives. Emmy didn't think she would feel so empty after such a big deal. All she could think about was the list of girls she knew had been with Ty. Sure, they'd become more popular. But she realized for the first time, and a little too late, they were all thinner than Emmy. They were all prettier than she was.

Ty's arms were around her. But all she could think about was how she'd tell her friends. Or would they somehow just magically know? Could you tell from looking when a girl had crossed that line?

At 6:17 in the morning, Emmy's phone buzzed. It was so loud it woke Ty before Emmy could find it in the depths of her big pleather purse. It was her mom. Emmy could tell she was frantic, even via text.

"Where the hell are you?"

Emmy was tempted to ignore it. Why should she answer? It was always the same thing anyway. Everything she did was wrong, so why even bother to try explaining?

The phone rang.

"Who is it?" Ty stretched and scratched his chest.

There was no way Emmy was going to talk to her mom with Ty right there, so she turned the phone to silent. Instead of answering, she texted back.

"Slept at Tiana's last night. Heading to school now. Sorry."

Instantly, a reply appeared.

"We need to talk. Tonight. Be there."

Her mom was quick on the draw, she'd give her that much.

Emmy put her phone in her bag. She managed

to doze for half an hour in Ty's arms. Then he woke her up and told her he needed to go home and change before school. She was tempted to do the same, but she knew if she went home she'd crawl into bed and her mom would add skipping school to the list of wrongs. Instead, she went alone to Stella's Café for an order of toast and jam.

At school, Emmy told her closest girlfriends, Michelle and Tiana, about her night. They looked at her like she was totally clueless.

"Ty Biggs is a disgusting pervert," Michelle said. "You should not be spending time with him. He fingered Rochelle right in Math class."

"Yeah, Emmy," Tiana agreed. "He's not quality."

"That thing with Rochelle was just a rumour," Emmy insisted. Somehow she'd convinced herself they'd be impressed. How could she have gotten it so wrong? Now all she wanted was a shower and a chance to start the day over.

"Why would Rochelle say it happened if it didn't?" Michelle asked. "I mean, girls don't make stuff like that up. Ty would. But Rochelle wouldn't."

Emmy didn't want to listen. Rochelle looked like a model and never talked to any of them.

"Yeah, Emmy," Tiana said again. "You can do better than Ty Biggs."

Easy for them to say, thought Emmy. Up to now, Emmy claimed to be holding out for someone special. Maybe Ty was an idiot, but he was willing to put his arms around her. For now, that was something.

02 The Realness

AFTER SCHOOL, EMMY SCURRIED HOME. She turned the key in the front door, opening it as quietly as she could. She tiptoed through the front hall to the sharp left that led to her room. She hoped no one was home.

"You worried your mom sick, you know," said a low and serious voice.

It was Ron. He was always up in her business.

"We worked everything out via text," Emmy said.

"Get your act together, missy, or your mom's going to lose it. Time to start being nicer to her."

Nicer to *her*? What the hell did Ron know? Emmy had spent years being more than nice to her mom. After Emmy's dad died, she practically stepped into his shoes. She stayed up late with her mother, letting her cry out her sorrows at the kitchen table. Ron knew nothing about that. He had swooped in just under a year ago and already they were all shacked up together. They played at being a perfect blended family with Ron's super annoying son, Brendan.

"We're talking later," she shot back. Why was Ron home all the time? Emmy closed her bedroom door firmly behind her.

There was no talk at dinner. Mom was on her tablet. Ron complained about Trudeau. Brendan did what he did best: nothing. When the time came for the dreaded talk with her mother, Emmy was back in her room. She was trying to tune out the smells and sounds seeping in from Brendan's room, a fourteen-year-old playing some kind of hard-core hip hop. The walls in Ron's old house were pretty thin.

The door opened a crack at first. Then it was pushed an arm's length.

"What are you doing?" Her mom stuck her head in.

Emmy shrugged. *Waiting for this very moment. Duh.*

"I know you weren't at Tiana's last night," her mom said. "Emmy, I know you spent the night with Ty. That's not the kind of life I want for you."

"You don't know anything about it."

"I went to school with Ty's mom's sister. They're a bunch of thugs, the whole family. I can tell you he's never going to love you or treat you well. He's using you."

"And your choices are so much better?" Emmy looked around. "Living in this weird man's house where nobody talks to each other?"

"Emmy, I work hard, okay? I'm tired at the end of the day. I've got a boss breathing down my neck and messaging me at all hours. I've got clients who expect an instant response. I can't just ignore them."

"But you can ignore me."

"You're blaming me for your bad behaviour? I'm at the end of my rope here, Emmy."

"If you work so hard, why do we have to live here?"

"We can't afford to live on our own. You remember how hard it was after your dad died. We were living on credit cards. Ron might not be your kind of guy and I know he's nothing like your dad. But he's got a steady job, he doesn't get drunk very often, and he's opened his home to us."

"Do you listen to yourself? You sound like a whore."

Her mom's hand came sweeping across Emmy's right cheek. Emmy kept on. "It's true. You can't make it on your own and that's why we're here. You don't love him. You have sex with him and he pays the bills."

"You don't know anything about love," her mom said angrily. "Especially if you think letting Ty Biggs paw at you makes him your boyfriend."

Emmy's eyes rolled backwards.

Her mother sighed and shook her head. "I could ground you, but you'll just sneak out. I could call Ty's family, but I don't want to talk to them. I really don't know what to do with you anymore."

"Maybe I should just leave," Emmy said huffily.

Her mom looked at her as if it was the first time. "Maybe you should," she said mildly.

That was not what Emmy was expecting to hear.

Emmy tore into a frenzy, grabbing her backpack and throwing the top layer of her laundry hamper into it. She couldn't squeeze the hodgepodge of colours, all knotted together, into the bag fast enough.

"Stop being dramatic," her mom said. "You're not going anywhere tonight."

Emmy wanted to slam the door, but her mom was still in her room. No one respected her space, her privacy. She needed to cry. She knew she would any second now. But there was no way the tears were going to flow in front of her mom. The one good thing that had come out of three years of hell was that she could hold back her tears.

"Get out!" Emmy yelled. "Leave me alone!"

In the morning, Emmy's mom was in the kitchen. She was running a latte through a pod. In Ron's house you didn't go to Starbucks. Starbucks came to you via Costco. The last of the steaming water spitted and sprayed into the mug.

Without making eye contact with Emmy, she said, "I spoke to your aunt Linda last night. You know you have a standing invite to stay with them in Vancouver."

"Since when? Why doesn't anyone tell me anything anymore?"

"Because you're hard to talk to."

"What about Paige?" She bet her mother didn't think Paige, Emmy's perfect cousin, was hard to talk to.

"Paige is still there. But Linda says they can make room for you."

"Well, what about school?" Emmy asked. Shouldn't her mom be the one asking practical questions like that?

"Distance ed."

"You really want to get rid of me, don't you?"

"Just laying some options on the table. Come on, Emmy. Help me out here."

"I haven't been to Vancouver since Dad died."

"I know. Maybe your dad is what all this is really about."

"Ugh, I'm so sick of being analyzed. Not everything is about that."

But Emmy wondered how things would be different if her dad was still around. It sucked to go down that rabbit hole of thinking. If her dad was there, they wouldn't be living with Ron. She'd have her own car, like he'd always promised her. Maybe she'd be a normal, well-adjusted teenager. Instead, here she was — a fat circus freak whose mom wanted to send her halfway across the country.

"Emmy, people are just trying to help you. Stop getting in the way of that."

"Whatever," Emmy said. Her mom was going to say and think whatever she wanted. No point trying to convince her of anything. But Vancouver? It was so far away — a different world, as far as Emmy could remember.

It was eerie how quickly her current life could vanish into thin air. Everything would disappear. Why was it so terrifying when things changed? Emmy knew that if this place was hell she should want to leave it. But now her instinct was to cling to what she knew. Michelle and Tiana weren't exactly her BFFs, but what if she had no one at all to hang out with? Wouldn't that be worse?

Emmy reached for the Lucky Charms in the cupboard. She poured some of the sugary cereal into a bowl, then drenched the fist-sized pile with milk. Brendan and Ron were in the other room. She could hear them laughing. Maybe they were laughing at her.

Emmy took a bite of the fruity, marshmallowy goodness. At least there would be cereal in Vancouver.

03 Never Go Home Again

AT SCHOOL, EMMY WANTED some alone time with Ty, but he was always surrounded by his pack and she was afraid to approach a group. He looked at her and she was sure he saw her. But he didn't make any move to even say hi. She texted him at lunch, but got no reply. She messaged him after school to tell him she was moving. Then she sat in her room, watching his comments appear beneath other peoples' photos.

Emmy felt hopeless. She couldn't even get a guy like Ty Biggs by blowing him. It was clear Winnipeg had nothing to offer her. There was no point in sticking around and becoming even more tragic. A fresh start in Vancouver would do her good. It was a chance to change herself completely.

A few days later, her mom helped her haul the big suitcase out to the driveway. With a one-two-three, they lifted it into the trunk of her mom's dented Pontiac Sunfire. The weight made the car sink down an inch or two. Emmy imagined the horror of having to carry it all by herself. She'd be landing in Vancouver International Airport, not on the tarmac of some lame little airstrip. The suitcase made her feel alone in the world.

"Do you have enough money on you?" her mom asked. She opened her purse. A gust of wind covered her mom's face with hair as she rummaged for a crumpled envelope and handed it to Emmy. "Here."

"What's this?" Emmy opened it to find a bunch of twenty-dollar bills. She didn't know how many and she didn't want to count them. "No, Mom, it's okay."

"Just take it. Some's from me. Some's from Ron."

"Oh." She almost said, 'money to get rid of me.' But she stopped herself. For all the horrible things about Ron, he was generous. "Tell him thanks."

"I will," her mom said.

Emmy opened the passenger door and sat down. When she looked over, she saw a tear streak down her mom's cheek.

"I just can't believe my baby's leaving."

"Mom, I haven't been your baby in a long time."

"You'll never get too old to be my baby. This is so much harder than I thought it would be. You get to get out, like you always wanted. You get to go on this great adventure. I just can't believe how hard it is to let you go."

Emmy rolled her eyes. "This whole thing was your idea."

"Calling your aunt last week was my idea. But you've been talking about leaving for a long time now. I finally figured, better you stay with your dad's family. You'll be in a place where I know you're safe instead of off in God Knows Where with Ty or some other guy like that."

On the freeway, Emmy's mom talked about practical stuff. "Have you got your passport?"

"Yes."

"Your anti-anxiety meds?"

"Yes."

"Prescription refill slips?"

"Yes."

"Glasses?"

"Of course."

"Toothbrush?"

"Mom!"

For the first time in ages, Emmy was in the right place, at the right time, doing the right thing. When she hugged her mom goodbye, Emmy was actually relaxed. She had almost forgotten what that felt like.

LOVE IS LOVE

Emmy lifted her suitcase from the carriage belt. Hauling that thing in her heavy coat into the Vancouver climate was making her sweat. She wiped her face before she went through the automatic glass doors. There was Paige, standing out against the crowd as usual. Her long, dark hair was in a side braid. She wore a black fedora and long, white t-shirt with a thin, gold chain dangling between her perfect breasts. Her parents stood behind her. The family was a portrait. Emmy thought about their first look at her, all pudgy and pasty. They must be dismayed at her size, her plainness, her mousy brown hair, and her pale freckled skin.

There were hugs all around. On the drive home, her aunt and uncle asked about the flight. Emmy caught them up on her mother, Ron, Ron's son, school. They turned right off Granville Street and then left on Main. Emmy's face was almost pressed against the car window. There were more restaurants and coffee shops than she remembered. Hipsters everywhere. As the car veered through the tree-lined side streets, Emmy wondered how she was supposed to fit in here. She had forgotten how different her uncle was from her dad, how different this family was from her own back in Winnipeg.

They climbed the narrow stairs to the second floor of the house, with Uncle Frank carrying the suitcase. Aunt Linda said, "I'm sure you've heard about the housing shortage in Vancouver. We had to get creative about your *room*."

"Don't worry," said Paige. "I decorated it. It's actually pretty cool."

Everything Paige did or touched or went near was always pretty cool.

Emmy followed her three hosts to the walk-in closet. It was not as small as the cupboard under the stairs that Harry Potter's aunt and uncle kept him in, but, by Winnipeg standards, it was not a room.

"Cute!" Emmy exclaimed, trying her best to sound grateful. But really she thought, *how can I possibly have a new life living in a closet?*

"I know it's small," her aunt said.

"But look," said Paige. "Shelves. And an adorable rice-paper lamp."

"I love it," Emmy said. "Thanks for letting me stay."

Emmy knew how hard they were trying to make her feel at home. But she didn't feel that way even when she was home. And it wasn't like moving to another city and living in a closet would make any difference. No matter where she went, she couldn't escape being herself.

"It's really no trouble," Frank said. His voice reminded her of her dad's.

Once she had the door closed, Emmy was surprised how safe she felt. Maybe it was her uncle's voice. Maybe it was the feeling that someone went to such trouble to make a place for her. She whipped out her notebook. By the light of the rice paper lamp, she scribbled that being in a closet was better than being in Ty's arms. She put her things on the shelves and felt them close around her. It was like being in a cocoon. Maybe, just maybe, staying here could turn her into a butterfly.

04 New Beginnings

EMMY WAS READY to turn in for the night. But outside her door, she heard her aunt pleading with Paige. "Would it kill you to spend a little time with her?"

A scoff. A mumble.

"Car privileges," her aunt said.

There was a knock at the closet door.

Paige was smiling a little too brightly. "Settling in okay? I was thinking we should go out. Up for it?"

Emmy looked at her phone. It was only 8:30 in Vancouver. But she was still on Winnipeg time, and to her body it was 10:30.

"I don't know," Emmy said.

"Come on," Paige urged. "It'll be fun."

In the driver's seat of the little red car, Paige adjusted the rear-view mirror. Emmy thought how perfect Paige looked, no matter how small the gesture.

They drove in silence for a while. Emmy looked out at the city. The yellow and orange leaves on the trees that lined Main Street cast the city in an amber glow. Emmy wondered if she would ever start taking Vancouver's beauty for granted.

Paige made a sharp right and parked in a no-parking zone. Emmy didn't say anything. She would never have let her mom get away with that back in Winnipeg.

"Let's see if Jude is working," Paige suggested.

"Jude?"

"You remember my friend Judy, from St. Mary's?"

Emmy remembered. "You're still friends?"

"Well, sort of. Yeah. I mean, we're still friends, but Judy's not Judy anymore. *He* goes by Jude." Paige raised her right eyebrow in Emmy's direction, looking for some sort of response. Emmy couldn't figure out what she was supposed to say, so she said nothing.

They crossed Broadway and walked into a café that looked like the set of a sitcom. Emmy took in the various event posters: poetry slams, indie bands, open mic nights, a performance series called That Hashtag. A familiar face looked up from behind the counter. He gave Paige a wave.

"Hi, Jude. This is my cousin, Emmy," Paige said. Emmy couldn't believe that Paige introduced them like they didn't even know each other. She wondered if the introduction was somehow related to Jude's gender. Did they need to be reintroduced as new people?

"Oh, hey. Yeah." Jude nodded and smiled at Emmy.

The smile nearly took Emmy's breath away. In front of her was the kind of guy she didn't know existed in real life. He looked like he should be on a stage, or better yet, a movie screen. He needed to be up where the lights would highlight his perfect face, and make the mystery in his chestnut-brown eyes deeper. Emmy found herself looking at his hands and trying to find the words she would write to describe them. They were the hands of an artist — no, a musician. Emmy wanted to write a scene of him sitting on the edge of her bed and playing a love song on the guitar just for her. He looked like if he were your boyfriend, he'd sit at the edge of your bed and play guitar or something.

His hair was shaved short on the sides and the top was slicked back to perfection, though he didn't seem like the kind of person who spent too long in front of a mirror. But the way his hair escaped his slicked-back 'do and fell in a few wispy strands around his face looked like it was done by a stylist. He dressed like he was one of the greasers from *The Outsiders*, in jeans and a white t-shirt with a lighter tucked into the roll of his sleeve.

When Jude fixed his dark eyes on her, Emmy was afraid she might disappear. She put up her hand to wave like a new girl at school being introduced at the front of the class. It was too formal. It was too casual.

"Hi," she said. "You're so hot now."

The words fell out of her by accident. Only when they were actually out there did she realize what she'd said. She talked quickly, as though more words might make him forget. "I mean hi. I mean, we met a few summers ago. I don't know if you remember."

"Sure I do," he said. "You guys sticking around?" He motioned with the rag he held, offering to wipe up a table.

"We'll hang out at the counter so we can harass you," Paige said.

Emmy followed her cousin to the counter. What she really wanted to do was bolt. She wanted to kick herself.

Jude looked at an order slip and got busy behind the espresso machine. Emmy tried to tell if he was taller than she was. Paige was much shorter than Emmy. She was much thinner too. Emmy was always horrified when she was the biggest person in a group.

"So, Emmy, aren't you from Saskatoon or somewhere?"

"Winnipeg."

Jude looked at her as though he expected her to say something more, but Emmy stayed silent. After that case of verbal vomit, she needed to have more control. But she couldn't look away from Jude. She didn't want to stare, but it seemed less risky than talking.

"So did you move or are you visiting?"

"Um . . . visiting?"

Emmy was desperate to come up with more than one-word answers. But she didn't believe that a guy like Jude would be interested in hearing what she had to say. Guys were never interested. Emmy had once been told by a friend that if you were going to be the fat girl, you had to at least have personality. Emmy was sure she didn't have that.

Jude stood tall, frothing milk into foam. Emmy looked him up and down, trying to get every detail so that she could write it down later. On his shirt, he wore a button with a picture of RuPaul. *What the hell?* Emmy thought she was the only person in the world who loved RuPaul. She thought about the nights after her dad died. Her mom was a mess and life was nothing but sad. The only thing that made it bearable was late-night reruns of *Drag Race*. She was pretty sure there was no one like RuPaul in Winnipeg, at least not at her school. But she had been drawn to the creativity, the sequins, the makeup, and the cattiness of the contestants. Mostly she loved how RuPaul talked about how you have to love yourself. She stared at the button and wanted to ask about it. But she was too uncertain of her words to say anything.

"A couple of Americanos, Jude," said Paige. She turned to Emmy.

"So they get in the coolest spoken-word poets and musicians to perform here," she explained. As if it wasn't totally clear to Emmy already that this was the place to be.

"Sounds cool," Emmy said. Cool in the way the poems in her notebook were not. She couldn't imagine her poems performed in front of a crowd of strangers.

Jude plunked a couple of small cups on saucers in front of them. Emmy really wanted to ask for cream to put in her coffee. Instead she stared at her cup like it was a gift that she didn't dare open. Paige stirred sugar into her cup and sipped.

Jude came back and placed two small pitchers in front of Emmy. "Sorry, I forgot because I know Paige drinks hers black. There's milk and cream for you."

Emmy watched the steam from her cup mist the steel surface of the cream pitcher as she poured.

When they were done, Paige stood up. She put on her jacket and said, "Let's get out of here, Emmy."

"Shouldn't we pay?" Emmy asked.

"Nah. We're good." She turned to her friend. "Right, Jude?"

"Of course. Get out of here."

"We should at least leave a tip then," Emmy said. She dug through her overstuffed bag in search of her wallet. Why were there so many candy wrappers and old receipts in there? What would people think if she were suddenly struck by a bus and a random stranger had to go through her bag in search of ID?

She put a five on the counter and followed Paige out the door.

05 Stay Away

BACK IN THE CAR, Emmy put on her seatbelt. She tried to sound casual, like she hadn't just met the hottest guy she'd ever seen. "Jude sure has changed a lot since last time."

"I know, right? Can you say 'awkward phase' or what?"

"I don't know, I think the changes really suit him."

"You would. Jude's a mess. But she organizes one of the city's most popular poetry nights. Even my TA knows about them, and he has, like, three books out."

"Wow. Is Jude a poet?"

"I don't frickin' know. Jude changes her mind every other week about everything under the sun. Right now I think she's busking and working on an album or something. But next week it'll be something else."

Emmy looked out the window. "Oh, look. Shoppers Drug Mart. Can we stop for a second? I forgot to bring shampoo."

Paige pulled into the parking lot and said she'd wait in the car. Emmy ran in. It should have reminded her of home. All the stores were supposed to be the same across the country. But she had to wander the aisles to figure out where to find the shampoo. On her way to the cash register, Emmy stopped and grabbed a box of chocolate chip cookies. She pounced on a bag of Old Dutch Rip-L chips. The chips were made in Manitoba and she needed something to make things seem normal again. Seeing Jude, making a fool of herself, she felt the kind of shame that could only be cured with potato chips.

In the comfort of her dark closet room, Emmy went over the evening. In her head, she pulled apart what she'd said and what she could do better next time. She thought about what other people said and what she thought they might have meant. Why did Paige disrespect Jude by calling him 'she'? And what was with not leaving a tip?

She opened the cookies and the chips, deciding she liked the combination of the two flavours together. Then she popped in her earbuds and listened to RuPaul. She imagined that at that very moment Jude was doing the same. Did Jude watch *Drag Race*? Or listen to RuPaul songs? Or obsess about MAC Cosmetics? The last question was unlikely, since there was nothing feminine about Jude at all. Maybe it didn't mean anything that Jude was wearing that button. Maybe it had come with the shirt. What were the odds that she and Jude idolized the same person?

Jude.

She couldn't stop thinking about him. She'd had crushes before, but nothing like this.

The next morning Emmy woke up unsure of the time. She thought about people trapped in small spaces waiting to be rescued and how odd it must be to pass the time like that. She reached for a chocolate chip cookie. Just one.

Downstairs she saw Paige already up. She was showered, made up, and dressed for a runway or a lecture hall.

"There's some smoothie left in the blender," Paige said.

"Thanks." Emmy poured the green mixture into a glass. There was definitely not enough to keep her stomach from growling. But she was afraid to ask Paige where they kept the cereal. Maybe no one here even ate cereal. Maybe that was why they were all so perfect. No gluten.

"So about Jude," Paige began. She put down her phone.

"Yeah?"

"She's a bit nuts, to put it lightly."

"What do you mean?"

"Well, I just . . . I feel a duty to tell you because I don't want to see you get hurt."

If there was such a thing as a full body blush, Emmy was feeling it. She felt naked and ashamed. Why did she have to comment on Jude's hotness? Did Paige know all about her insta crush?

"I'm not . . . I don't . . ." Emmy stammered. But she couldn't complete the sentence.

"Jude's not the kind of person you want to get mixed up with. She's really good at getting people to do things for her."

Emmy looked at her cousin, trying to decode what she meant. Instead of reacting to Paige's comment, she asked, "Why are you saying *her* and *she* today when you said *his* and *him* when we were at the café?"

"What does it matter? That's just the beginning of the strange cocktail that is Jude."

"Okay?" Emmy looked at her phone and scrolled through social media. She looked frantically for something to turn the conversation to. Kardashian news. Bieber fever gone bad. Anything.

"Jude's been up to some bad shit lately. Like, I'm not going to get into it, but there are people involved. People you don't want to know."

"I thought you weren't going to get into it."

"Emmy, there's a lot that could go wrong for you in this city."

"Vancouver, the hotbed of criminal activity."

Paige was not amused by Emmy's sarcasm. As she pushed her chair out, she said, "I'm just saying."

"I'll consider myself warned," Emmy said.

Emmy longed to know what it was that Jude had done to get such a reputation. He seemed charming and smart. She couldn't imagine Jude doing anything really bad. Not hurting people. Theft, maybe? How mysterious.

Paige threw some books into her backpack. Phone in hand, she turned back to Emmy. "Got plans for the day?"

"I'll settle in. Maybe do some homework."

"Mom and Dad will be home around six. I'll probably be home after them."

Paige seemed to have forgotten all about Jude. She told Emmy to feel free to use any of her makeup. She said that they could raid her closet together, like she was promising a treat to a child.

Alone, Emmy went through the cupboards. She found some oatmeal and a pot and made herself a real breakfast. *What kind of people live on green drinks?* she wondered.

She walked slowly through the living room. She glanced at the photos of Paige at various stages of her glamorous life and a few awkward ones of herself. She hovered for a long time over one of her dad holding her on his shoulders. She was a toddler and had her arms wrapped around his head. She didn't remember the day itself, but felt like she did because she'd seen the picture so many times. Emmy didn't need to cry over the picture. Not anymore. Not today, anyway.

She spread her textbooks out on the table and opened her clunky old laptop. Before she knew it, it was noon and high time for lunch and a nap. By three o'clock, she still hadn't done anything. She figured she should work somewhere she might be forced to concentrate. What about the café? Emmy thought about Paige warning her away from Jude. But the café was the only spot in the whole city that Emmy knew.

06 Fly Tonight

EMMY GOT DRESSED and looked at herself in the mirror. Then she got undressed and started over. This went on until her bed was covered with a pile of clothing. It looked like laundry except that it was clean.

She went into Paige's room, but she couldn't bring herself to open the closet. The dresser looked like something in a movie star's dressing room. It had a mirror attached and a gazillion lipsticks and compacts and eyeliners. Looking at her pasty reflection, Emmy delved in. She squirted a thin layer of BB cream onto her fingers and smeared it beneath her cheekbones. It was darker than her skin, but she figured it would work as a contour. She thought some dramatic black eyeliner and smoky neutral shading would make her look like Adele. She didn't nail it, but she wasn't Adele. At least the face looking back from the mirror was going for glamour.

Emmy brushed her hair. She looked at the mousy brown shoulder-length locks, and twisted her hair into an updo using a bunch of Paige's black bobby pins to hold it in place. While she was at it, why not help herself to some perfume? And a quick-drying coat of nail polish?

By the time Emmy was out the door, it was almost time for her aunt and uncle to be home. She texted them and said she'd be back after dinner. She walked through the charming neighbourhood until she reached Main Street. A soap shop had a display of hand lotion out on the sidewalk, so she tried one of the samplers. Another shop had furniture in the windows. She looked at the prices. She'd have to spend an entire year of her life working at some minimum-wage job just to buy a sofa. But even thoughts about money couldn't ruin her good mood.

She turned onto Broadway and strolled into the café. Jude was laughing, surrounded by a crowd of girls. It was just the way Emmy remembered Ty, always with an entourage of gigglers. Just as Emmy had decided to turn and bolt, the horde of girls put on their coats. Too late. When Jude called out his goodbyes, he saw Emmy framed in the café door. "Emmy," he said. "You're here." He didn't sound surprised. It was almost like he was expecting her. And was it possible? He seemed happy to see her.

"What can I get you?" Jude asked.

"I don't know."

"Cheesecake?"

"I haven't had dinner yet."

"Then you have to. It's the best appetizer."

Emmy laughed. What a line. "Okay, sure. And an Americano?"

Emmy sat at a table by the window. Scanning the room and the people walking by outside was fun. But it was impossible to turn her attention away from Jude for very long. He stood out in ways she had never seen before. Whatever it was, there was more to Jude than his slender frame and his slightly swaggering manner. Emmy wanted to write about it. She even had her notebook open in front of her. But she didn't have the words to even start describing him.

When he brought out her coffee, Emmy blurted, "Can I be super awkward?"

"Always," Jude said.

"Do you prefer 'they' as a pronoun?"

After Paige's rudeness, Emmy had turned to the Internet. Most of the blogs and posts by trans people said that the best thing to do is ask. Logical enough. But in the moment, it was terrifying. She felt that any question she asked could offend Jude.

Jude's eyes met Emmy's. He smiled. "I like 'he,'" he said quietly. "And thanks for asking."

Emmy looked back down at her notebook.

Jude's eyes followed hers. "What do you have there?"

Emmy hesitated. Her instinct was to hide her writing. But she adjusted the notebook to let him see. "Just some poems."

"You're a poet? You should perform tonight for That Hashtag. I could totally squeeze you in."

"That's okay. I'm not very good. I wouldn't call myself a poet."

"I call myself a musician and I can't read music."

"Yeah, but that's you."

"And that means?"

"I don't know. You're . . . convincing."

"I guess I'll take that as a compliment."

"It is one." Emmy blushed.

Once he left, she wondered if what she felt was anything like being drunk. He had asked her to perform. He had confidence in her without even reading her poetry. It was the most exciting thing that had happened to her in ages. Maybe ever.

When he brought the cheesecake, Jude paused at the table. "You *have* to read tonight. On stage."

"Me? No. Never."

"Why not? It'll be fun."

Emmy wanted to say that getting up in front of a group of people and exposing her feelings to the world didn't sound like fun. It was more like her worst nightmare. But she didn't say that.

"It *would* be fun," she said.

"All right, it's settled," Jude said. He looked at her a little longer than was comfortable. Emmy tried not to stare into his eyes. She tried to ignore his long lashes. "You're helping me out," Jude went on. "A bunch of people bailed last minute. It's a Vancouver thing."

"Bailing?"

He nodded and walked away before she could respond.

07 Main Event

EMMY WATCHED AS TWO GIRLS came in the front door of the café. One had a nose ring and short hair. The other had a long, purple mane with purple lipstick to match. Emmy watched them try to hug Jude. She decided she liked how he backed away with his hands up like he was defending himself from fans. She hoped the girls weren't also poets. They were a million times cooler than she was.

Emmy noticed Jude was much louder around the

purple girl than he was around her. It was like his charm could be turned up and down like the volume on a phone. Emmy ate her cheesecake and felt like leaving. It was all too much to feel rejected before anything had even happened.

Starting to plan her getaway, Emmy noticed a tall woman standing by the door. She was beautiful, dressed in black with fishnet stockings and high-heeled boots. Her tight mini-dress revealed a figure so perfect it almost hurt Emmy to think about it. It did hurt when she saw Jude go to greet the dark goddess and lead her to a table. They spoke quietly. Jude gave her a pat on the shoulder when he got up to start the show. Before Emmy could act on her plan to leave, Jude turned on the spotlight over the tiny stage. The place was packed. It got even more crowded when a group of guys rolled in, drunk and loud. They were all much taller than Jude, who was working alone while the other barista was out for a smoke. They asked Jude for beer.

When he asked them to leave, the tallest guy looked at Jude and said, "There's no way a little pansy like you could make us go."

"You're right," Jude said. "And since there are three of you and only one of me, that makes this whole thing unfair and lame. Do you want to be unfair and lame?"

They grumbled, but left.

Emmy had been clutching her notebook so tightly her sweaty palms curled the paper book into a roll. She let out a huge sigh of relief when they left. Jude went back to being Jude. The other barista came back. He dimmed the lights and moved some chairs around. Jude grabbed the lighter from the fold in his shirt sleeve and lit candles. He rose up on the stage, staring out at the adoring faces in the crowd.

"Guys, gals, and everyone in between," he began. "Tonight's That Hashtag is going to be amazing. We've got a great line-up from across the country."

He introduced the woman in black as Clarisse, the voice of That Hashtag. Gliding like an elegant swan, the woman made her way to the stage. She thanked everyone for coming and Jude for organizing. She said that this reading was taking place on her ancestors' land and she wanted to honour them. And then she began her poem. It was a sensual description of the cold, empty darkness of the city's streets and the brightness of the sunrise. Emmy was so caught up in the words and images that she forgot everything else around her.

Suddenly, Jude was back on the stage. He looked right at Emmy and winked. She felt her entire face go pink. Her palms were sweaty. She thought if she wasn't careful she might actually poop her pants. Her stomach was in such knots that she didn't think she could stand.

"From Winnipeg to Vancouver, Emmy has moved people with her heartfelt poetry. Let's give her a big rain-city welcome. Get on up here, girl."

Emmy almost cringed as the applause washed over her. Why did Jude introduce her as if she'd done this sort of thing before? And to have to follow Clarisse? It was sheer terror. She stood to walk to the stage, but it was like she could only move in slow motion. Her notebook was heavy in her arms.

"Uh . . . hi," Emmy managed, looking out at the crowd. Hip big-city people stared back at her. They all waited for something to happen. Emmy cracked open her notebook to the poem she had chosen and practiced for the last two hours. It was the one she'd imagined reading to Ty, the one about feeling alone. She looked at the short poem, only five lines. Suddenly she decided that it was stupid, the worst poem ever written.

Emmy flipped the pages of her notebook. What should she read? Finally she stopped at a poem she had written for English class. It was about the springtime slush that lined Winnipeg streets and how it revealed all the secrets of winter as it melted. It had earned her her first A and a glowing comment from her English teacher, so Emmy had torn the page out of her Hilroy notebook and pasted it into this book. She realized she felt a lot safer going with something she knew had pleased at least one person. Especially since that person was supposed to know what she was talking about.

Emmy began to read her poem. It was a sonnet written in the style of Shakespeare. That was the assignment.

When Emmy got to the line that rhymed *brown* with *drown*, the audience laughed. When she got to the next rhyme, they laughed even harder. Cheesecake rumbled around inside of Emmy. By the time she finished what she had written as a very sad poem, everyone there was in stitches.

Jude, applauding, came up to take the mic. He smiled, which made it worse. Emmy ran off the stage and into the washroom, where she emptied out the contents of her guts.

As Emmy collected her things from her table, she glanced up at the stage. The purple girl was crooning a song while strumming her guitar. There was no point in saying goodbye to Jude. If all went well, she'd never have to face him again.

Emmy left quickly, as though a faster pace would

help her erase the memory of the sound of people laughing at her. She crossed the street and stopped in at the Shoppers. She headed straight for the refrigerator. She needed orange juice, a sandwich, a tub of rice pudding, and some chocolate milk. For good measure, she also grabbed a bag of honey mustard potato chips while she waited at the checkout.

08 Turning Tables

EMMY OPENED HER EYES, not sure where she was. She turned on the light and looked at the stash of empty food wrappers piled up like a fortress around her. She could practically hear her mom explaining to her aunt that Emmy would comfort eat when her anxiety got the better of her.

There was nothing worse than the way her mom thought she understood her. She really had no clue. And there was something so hurtful about the term 'comfort eating.' Emmy remembered how she'd wake up at night and hear the TV still on. Her dad would be in the living room, passed out. Beer cans would be spread out in front of him. She'd take the remote from his hand and turn off the TV. Sometimes he'd wake up and be confused about where he was. Then he'd smile at her warmly and they'd make ice cream sundaes as he told her to keep it secret.

Emmy's mom always blamed her for the missing ice cream. But Emmy never said anything about how it had disappeared in the middle of the night, stolen spoonful after stolen spoonful. Now she wondered if her mom had ever accused her dad of comfort eating. Thinking about her messed-up parents was better than thinking about her gigantic failure as a poet.

Downstairs, she found Paige drinking the last of her green smoothie and idly thumbing through her phone.

"Morning," Paige chirped. "Heard about your big debut last night."

"You what? My what?"

"Jude texted me this photo."

Paige flashed her phone at Emmy. There she was, the light over the stage making her look like an uncooked breakfast sausage.

"Oh, God," Emmy said.

"I can't believe you didn't invite me."

"It just sort of happened. I didn't plan it."

"Still."

Paige seemed genuinely pissed off to have been left out.

Emmy didn't know what to say. "Honestly, I kind of wish it hadn't happened at all," she finally admitted.

"Why?"

"Because it sucked, that's why."

There. She said what Paige wanted and needed to hear. Emmy admitted that she accepted her role as the loser of the family, that she was a horrible failure and doomed to walk in Paige's shadow.

Paige's face seemed calmer. "I'm sure it wasn't *that* bad."

"It was terrible."

"You should have let me help you with your outfit and hair. Spotlights can be so unforgiving. That peachy shirt really washes you out, you know. Does nothing for your complexion." Paige analyzed the photo.

Which is worse? Emmy wondered. *To be on stage with strangers gawking at me or right here in Paige's kitchen getting her fashion advice? Tough call.*

But soon Paige got bored and started talking about herself again. She told Emmy about her busy day. She was going to have to talk to her TA after seminar. And it was going to be awkward because of the big crush he had on her. Emmy tuned out about the time Paige was saying how obvious it was that he liked her because he could barely look at her in class.

Emmy wondered what it was like to have that sort of confidence. She had never in her life believed that anyone liked her, especially guys, even if they said they did. It just wasn't the sort of thing that was believable. But she couldn't fault Paige. After all, it was totally believable that guys would fawn all over her. She was pretty and thin. She walked well and dressed well. She was always in the centre of things, where the party was.

"So anyway, I'm probably going to the pub after class," Paige finished.

"Cool."

"What are you doing? Hanging out here?"

"Well, yeah. I have school work to do."

"Don't we all?"

Emmy nodded.

Paige put on her coat and ran her hands behind her head to pull her long luscious hair out of the collar. It bounced behind her as she walked toward the door.

"Ta!" Paige said over her shoulder.

"Bye."

Alone with her thoughts, Emmy decided that there were two types of girls in the world. There were girls who could use their looks and charms to get ahead, and girls like Emmy.

Just as Emmy was finishing the dinner dishes, Paige came through the front door.

"We saved you some quinoa salad and a black-bean burger," Uncle Frank said to her.

"I already ate."

Of course she did, Emmy thought. *She probably ate an apple at four o'clock and is still full from it.*

"Emmy, get dressed. Let's get out of here," Paige said.

"What? Why?" Emmy was in her pink fleece pajamas and didn't want to change.

"Just do it. Let's go."

Emmy set the last plate to dry in the dish rack and wiped her hands on the fancy towel that hung on the oven door. Upstairs, she put on a black outfit that was supposed to be slimming, according to Paige. Paige commanded Emmy into her bedroom, sat her down in front of the girly dresser and did her makeup. Emmy felt good having someone touch her face, even if she was afraid of the result.

When they entered the café, Paige ran up to Jude.

Emmy noticed he tensed up when she kissed him on each cheek. Emmy looked down.

"Emmy, don't let Paige turn you into her Mini Me," Jude said.

"What?"

"That." He made a circle in front of Emmy's face, pointing at her lips. "It doesn't suit you."

Emmy wanted to disappear. If there was a trap door that led to a pit of alligators, she would choose to fall into it. Jude criticizing her hurt more than anything else.

"Hush now. She looks great," Paige said. Emmy thought Paige seemed more loyal to the makeup than to her.

The bright red lipstick that Paige had insisted on seemed to weigh on Emmy's lips. She licked her lips trying to get it off. She couldn't help it. She had read somewhere that women ate an average of eight pounds of lipstick over a lifetime. That had grossed her out, but now she didn't care.

"So anyway, last night was fun," Jude said to Emmy.

"Was it?" Emmy asked. "I didn't ruin it?"

"What do you mean? You got quite a few laughs."

"They were just laughing *at* me."

"Well, the rhyme scheme probably threw people off."

"It was a sonnet. They rhyme."

"Didn't people stop writing those in like the eighteen hundreds or something?"

"Not in my English class."

"So that's not how you normally write?"

Emmy shook her head.

"Then why'd you read that one?" Jude asked.

"I don't know. I got nervous."

Emmy never told people stuff like that. She thought it made her seem weak. But Jude seemed to get it. He gave her a kind nod and held her gaze.

"Next time share what's in your heart. It won't fail because it's obvious you have a good one."

"You don't know that," Emmy said.

"Oh, but I do. Don't think I forgot about all the times you put up with this one's bitchy friends." Jude glanced at Paige. "Remember how they used to hate on everyone's taste in music, clothes . . . guys."

"So anyway," Paige said in an exaggerated way, glaring as though a single look of disapproval could erase the past. "There's a group of us going to the park later. You coming, Jude?"

Emmy wondered how she'd make her exit. There was no way Paige was going to ask her to come along. It would be rude to tag along without being welcome. But it'd also be rude to just leave.

"Who's going?" Jude asked.

Paige listed off a bunch of names. Emmy watched her cousin, admiring her skill in the art of getting people to do things they didn't want to do. She ended with a smile and told Jude, "Everyone wants to see you."

"What the hell. Why not?" Jude said. Then he turned to Emmy. "You're going, right?"

"Me?"

"Yeah, you." He smirked.

She decided that she would let them all off the

hook by coming up with an excuse. Jude didn't need some high school girl cramping his style.

"Uh . . ."

"Of course you're coming," Jude said.

Emmy couldn't refuse him. "I guess I am."

09 Sweetest Devotion

"DUDE CHILLING PARK? Is it really called that?" Emmy asked as they approached. The place was lit with lots of street lamps, but the lights cast weird shadows. To Emmy, playgrounds at night looked like horror movies.

"Yep."

"What the hell?"

"Some artist person made a sign calling it Dude Chilling Park and the city removed it. But people around here liked it and petitioned the city to keep it, so they did," Jude explained.

"Vancouver is seriously awesome." There was no way that would have happened back in Winnipeg.

Jude shrugged.

Across the grounds, a crowd of people was making a lot of noise. A big white cloud hung above them, letting off the skunky smell that made Vancouver famous.

Paige walked ahead, like the tip of a pyramid, leading Emmy and Jude into the larger group. When she got close, she burst forward in a run. She opened her arms to grab people into a huge group hug.

"Yay!" She squealed. It was like she was reuniting with long lost friends. "Everyone, this is my cousin, Emmy."

They waved like good obedient folks, but nobody seemed to care. There were a lot of blank expressions. Emmy knew the look. She'd seen enough of it in the smoke pit behind the school back in The Peg. She wondered how Jude felt in places like this, around people like that.

Paige jumped into the action right away. She grabbed a guy with dreadlocks pulled up into a man-bun and wildly signalled to him. He took her by the hand and told her to relax. He sat her on his lap, facing him and put her arms around him. Then he fiddled with something in his bag.

It was strange for Emmy to watch her perfect cousin take a drag from a joint in a park. Emmy didn't judge people who drank or smoked . . . anything. Live and let live. But it was weird to see someone as thin and competitive and clear-skinned as Paige do it. Didn't she get the munchies?

They passed the joint around. When it came to Emmy, she held it to her lips. She turned her head up to the stars while looking away from the crowd, then passed it to Jude.

"I'm good," he said, passing it along.

"What now?" Emmy asked.

"I think you're looking at it," Jude told her.

"Want to go sit down?"

"Yeah," Jude said. "How about over there?" He

pointed at a spot away from the crowd.

It was perfect. Emmy did not care about making friends with all these people. But a chance to sit next to Jude? Now that was something.

"I wish you had your guitar," she told him. "I'd love to hear you play."

"I've got a harmonica."

"Get out."

"No, really," he said, digging around in the inside of his jacket. "Never be without some way of making music. That's my motto."

"Good one."

Emmy watched intently as Jude played. She committed each precious moment to memory. She had never been serenaded before. Not that that was what this was. She was sure Jude was just doing it to be nice. But still, how dreamy.

"It's like we're hopping the rails or something," she said.

He laughed. "You weirdo."

"Am I weird?"

"The best people are." His eyes told her he was teasing her playfully, not meanly. He was flirting.

What was the right way to respond? Emmy asked herself. Her belly flopped. For a moment, she thought she would hurl. There was nothing to do but quickly change the subject.

"Oh, my God. Look!" she pointed at one of Paige's friends who was twirling around and around. Her friends all fell over around her, laughing.

Jude shook his head. "They've been like this for years. I don't know what Paige sees in them. Except maybe that she doesn't have to try as hard as she usually does."

"You think she tries hard?"

"Sure. You don't get the kind of fan club she's got without trying."

"I guess. She makes it look effortless, though." Emmy looked at her cousin, who was laughing, but still standing.

Emmy and Jude sat side by side. Neither of them said anything, and a silent awkwardness grew around them. Emmy leaned against Jude's arm, thinking he might shove her away, even playfully. But he didn't. He absorbed the lean.

"Can I ask you something?" he finally said.

"Anything," Emmy said.

"Are you queer?"

The question sent her mind spinning. Was he asking because he could see she had a crush on him? Did a crush on him mean that she was queer? "Not, um, officially, I don't think."

"You've never kissed a girl? Or been attracted to one?"

She shook her head.

"So when you look at me, you see me as, like, a guy?" Emmy could see it was a risky question, even for someone as confident as Jude. She heard the nervousness in his voice.

"Well, that's what you are. Isn't it?"

The sides of Jude's lips curled downward, although he was clearly smiling, not frowning. He got a faraway look in his eyes and seemed almost tearful.

"Where did you come from?"

Emmy knew better than to answer the question.

After a period of silence, Jude said, "It's cool being here with you. I come here alone sometimes."

"You do?" But Jude was always surrounded by a posse of admirers. Wasn't he? Emmy's mind had been taken over by thoughts of Jude ever since that first night at the coffee shop. But she was starting to see she didn't really know him.

"I come to think, be by myself. That kind of thing." Jude looked off at the trees.

"Really?"

"Why are you so surprised?" he asked. "I've been coming to this exact spot since middle school. I grew up with a big family, a busy house, always bustling. Mostly I loved that. Totally thrived on it. But now and then I had to be alone. Gather my thoughts. You know?"

"Totally." Home seemed far away. She just wanted to listen to Jude.

10 Snapshot

AUNT LINDA HAD TAKEN PAIGE out to get their nails redone. Emmy imagined having a mom with friends who did professional acrylics at cost. They were getting eyelash extensions too. Emmy thought about how her mom's idea of a beauty routine was a discount lipstick from the grocery store.

Instead of being glamorous, Emmy planned to spend her Vancouver Saturday afternoon pretty much as she would have back in The Peg. She was sipping on a hot chocolate, lounging in her fleece pants in front of the TV when her Uncle Frank came into the room.

"No plans, eh?" he joked. "Me neither. What are you watching?"

"Just something lame on Netflix. I don't even know what it is." The truth was she hadn't really been watching. She'd been obsessing over Jude, replaying their conversation over and over. She thought about better answers to his questions and what she wanted to say next time. She was hoping there'd be a next time. She daydreamed about leaning into Jude, recalling the magnetic pull of his shoulder.

"Want to go for a bike ride?" Uncle Frank asked.

"That's kind of random."

"I'm going if you want to ride along. We have a few bikes in the garage. My wife and daughter don't use them."

"I'll go," Emmy said, surprising herself. *First a poetry reading and now this? Weird.*

She had been toying with the idea of starting to work out, but hadn't taken the first step. *This might be just the thing*, she thought to herself. She went into her closet, quickly slipped off the pink fleece pants and threw on the best thing she could think of to ride in — her jeans.

Riding behind her uncle, Emmy took in the sight of well-maintained old houses and the odd one that looked like it should be torn down. They huffed and puffed their way up the Ontario Bikeway. She saw signs for Queen Elizabeth Park. Her thighs were killing her. Each rotation of the tires was torture.

They finally stopped. Emmy stood, gasping for breath. Her uncle handed her a water bottle. As she took a big swig, she felt some of it leak out of her mouth. That was just a dribble compared to the sweat that ran off her.

"Look," Uncle Frank said, gesturing out at the horizon.

Below them, the city sparkled under the setting sun. Streetlights glittered in the dusk. Downtown, with all its glass towers, gleamed.

"Wow," Emmy said.

"You know, your dad and I used to come here when we were growing up."

"You did?"

The thought that her father had stood in that exact spot and looked out at that same view made her tearful.

"Things were different then, of course," Uncle Frank said. "But things are always changing."

Emmy thought of Jude, how he'd like what her uncle just said. She wanted to remember the line exactly to tell Jude about this very moment. But she knew she wouldn't be able to say it in a way that could make him feel how she felt right now. She wanted to write down her uncle's words so she could remember them. But instead she took out her cell phone and took a panorama photo.

"It's okay to ask me about your dad," her uncle said. "I want you to know that."

"Thanks. That means a lot to me."

"Well, it means a lot to me that you came out with me. I think it's great having you here. I like that you like bike riding."

"I don't, really."

"I'll ask you again at home. Downhill is the fun part."

They put their water bottles away and headed down. He was right. The wind in her hair and the lack of effort made biking home more like a ride at a fair. It was like flying. Emmy wanted to tour the city this way. She suddenly realized she had the freedom to do that.

Back at the house, Emmy ran up to her room. She tore through her notebook, as if she couldn't get to a blank page fast enough. She quickly penned down the scene as she remembered it. *Standing above it all, no longer alone, separation no longer matters — aren't we looking at the same sunset?*

She looked again at the photo on her phone. It captured how the scene appeared. But in her notebook, she had recorded how it *felt*. Only a few weeks before, she never would have ridden a bike. She never would have felt the need to write the way she just did. Emmy knew that she was changing.

Once again, her thoughts turned to Jude. He had transformed himself. So could she. Emmy could let go of the girl she'd been and become the person she knew she was meant to be.

After showering and changing back into her fleece pants, Emmy joined her uncle in the den. He was reading a thick book when she walked in.

"Do you miss him?" she asked.

"My brother? All the time."

He gestured for her to sit down.

"What was he like when he was my age?" Emmy asked as she sat in a comfy armchair.

"Let's see now. You're seventeen. He was, well . . . when he was that age he was pissed off at everything. Our parents, the world. He was really into grunge music. He even thumbed it down to Seattle, hoping to meet his idol, Kurt Cobain. He was crushed when Cobain died."

"He liked Kurt Cobain? He never told me that."

"You know who Kurt Cobain is?" Frank seemed impressed.

"I have Spotify."

"You're pretty cool for a teenager."

"Thanks."

"You want to see some of his notebooks? Your dad's, not Kurt's."

"He wrote notebooks? And you have them? Um, hell yes."

"I kept them for you. I didn't want to give them to you until I knew you were interested."

"I am."

Emmy followed her uncle upstairs. He spread apart a foldable ladder right underneath a square on the ceiling. The attic was where her family had stayed that summer way back when. She had wondered why she wasn't put up there again, but now she got it. There was a bunch of stuff up there. Maybe way more than notebooks. Frank climbed up the ladder and slid the ceiling square up and over. He hoisted himself into the attic. Moments later, Emmy held two hardcover notebooks that said 'Property of George.'

"Oh, my God."

"They're pretty dark. Your father had a lot of demons."

Emmy nodded and clutched the books to her chest. "Mind if I go into my room for a while?"

"Go ahead. I don't know how you can stand to be in there."

"I like it."

"George would have liked it too."

Emmy held the books in her hands. They were precious, a gift from a past that she had assumed was lost forever. She had thought she would never learn more about her dad, from her dad. She had known that their conversations were over, but sitting there, cross-legged, with his words in her lap, Emmy felt his presence. It wasn't ghostly. It felt real.

She rifled through the pages. She landed on random lines in her dad's messy handwriting. "Why do I want what I can't have?"

She couldn't help but cry and she didn't want

to risk tears falling on the pages. So she clutched the notebooks and lay down with them. She cradled them to her chest like she had once done with her teddy bear that wasn't really a bear but a parrot that she loved until it was a mangled mess of fluff.

When Emmy finally made her way downstairs, she found Aunt Linda setting the table around trays of take-out. Paige sat slouched in her chair, looking at her phone.

Uncle Frank came to the table. "Hey, Paige," he said, "Do you know who Kurt Cobain is?"

"Uh, one of your clients?" she answered without even looking up.

"Yeah, that's right." He cast a wink in Emmy's direction.

Emmy laughed. Paige didn't even notice, which made it all the funnier. Emmy hoped Uncle Frank would not mention the notebooks to Linda and Paige at dinner, and he didn't. She had a feeling she was the only one he would ever tell about them.

11 Melt My Heart to Stone

HOLDING THE NOTEBOOK to her chest, Emmy headed to Dude Chilling Park for some solitude. If Jude was able to find peace there, maybe she could, too. She went with no expectations. Well, that wasn't true. She half expected to get a glimpse into Jude's world, to see things as he did. But then she saw Jude. He was sitting on the bench they had shared, exactly where she'd pictured him.

"What are you doing here?" he asked.

"You said it was a good place to come and think, so . . ." She shrugged.

He looked at the books cradled in her arms. "Your writing?"

Emmy was nervous. "No, uh, my dad's."

"Too bad. I was going to ask you to read me something. Would you do that some time?"

His request left her totally mute. She was taken aback by his interest. The fantasy of reading her work to a guy was one thing. She'd had that many, many times, with Ty and with quite a few different fictional guys. But the reality was scary. Was Jude ready? Was she?

"Join me?" Jude asked.

She sat down beside him like a tame old dog. It was too soon to tell Jude about her dad, too soon to read him a poem. It was too soon to feel like Jude was the only person in the world who might ever understand her.

They sat quietly for a while. Then Jude suddenly said, "Everyone else I've ever met feels like they have to talk or like they need me to talk. It's cool you're not like that."

"People think I'm shy, but I'm . . . I'm just quiet."

"Well, it's nice. I've heard about it before, you know. When people can be quiet together. But I've never experienced it. I like it."

"You do?" She smiled, then tried to hide it.

Jude looked down at his sketchbook. He penciled in some shade along the sides of the tree he'd been drawing. Emmy opened one of her dad's notebooks, but she couldn't concentrate. She stared at the margins and his handwriting without actually reading the words. It was enough in this moment to know the notebooks existed and that her uncle had kept them safe for her. She had a lifetime ahead of her to understand them. Besides, she was distracted by how close she was to Jude.

Across the park, Emmy noticed a kid whose mom had a bag of brightly coloured balls. The little girl threw one ball into the air and then another, like she was trying to teach herself to juggle.

"Look!" Emmy said.

Jude laughed along with the child's clumsy attempts to grab each fallen ball.

Emmy noticed the way Jude held back. It seemed like he wanted to join them, but was cautious. She nudged him. "Go on," she said.

Jude got up from their bench and went to the kid. "I'm Jude," he said. "Some folks call me Jude-the-Dude. Juggling expert. At your service." He tipped his hat to the mom who was breastfeeding a little one beneath a polka-dotted sheet.

"I'm Shandy," said the four-year-old after getting a nod from her mom.

"Can I show you how?" asked Jude.

Jude tossed the blue and red balls in the air — first two, then three. They bounced in the air as though they were moving around on their own. Shandy laughed and clapped her tiny hands together.

"Can you pick up the green one and toss it to me?" Jude asked.

Shandy used both hands to throw the ball to him. Jude absorbed it into the growing circle of colour in front of him. The mom on the bench made a surprised sound. Several people gathered around.

Emmy loved the way Jude commanded an audience. She saw how gentle he was with Shandy and thought he'd make a great dad someday. He was as natural with the little girl as he was with the crowd at the café.

Finally, the balls fell to the ground. Shandy begged Jude to get them going again. This time, he got her to throw all of them to him. The crowd around them had grown to a full circle of spectators. Most were people who had been sitting or strolling. But a group on bikes who'd stopped for a swig of water got caught up in the moment too.

To Emmy it was like being in the middle of a human interest story on the news. She felt like she had had stumbled upon someone swimming with otters. It was awesome.

When the mom announced that it was time to go, Jude got Shandy to take a bow and the crowd went wild. A couple of people pressed bills into Jude's palm.

"You're amazing," Emmy said as they walked out of the park together.

Jude shrugged. "I'm glad I saw you today. I never

would have had the courage to do that alone. And I didn't know how much I needed it."

Emmy paused as they neared her street. "I'm going this way."

She was hoping for a hug goodbye, but Jude didn't even slow his pace. She grabbed him by the arm. He stopped and turned. They were face to face. It was now or never.

"It was great to spend time with you," Emmy said, hating how the words sounded as soon as they were out of her mouth. She opened her arms.

"I'm not a hugger," Jude said quickly. "Sorry. Issues."

Oh, no! "No, no. Me either. I was just stretching," she explained. She stretched her arms out as wide as they could go to prove it. "Well, I'll see you around, I guess."

She turned to go. Instinct told her to run, but that would be uncool. So, she just walked away in shame.

"See you," she heard Jude say to her retreating back.

12 Cover Girl

IN THE PRIVACY OF THE DARKNESS of her closet-room, Emmy googled Jude, then Jude-the-Dude, and Jude-the-Dude and Vancouver and juggling. The image search didn't reveal much at all. There were other ways of getting what she needed. She searched singers now that she knew purple girl's name. She had to scroll through a nightmare of selfies of pretty girls, an avalanche of shoes and food. And then . . . jackpot. Jude. He was tagged. She clicked on it, but he had set his account to private. At least now she had his online handle.

Hours passed as Emmy moved through a maze of unknown faces. She collected a few sightings and the first ideas of the kind of person Jude was when he was not at work or at the park. It was almost impossible to read him through the images. It made him all the more intriguing. What could you make of close-ups of his hands, a shot of him on a bike, and a picture of him pointing at a sandwich board: *What pronouns does a chocolate bar use? Her/she.* He looked like he was having a good laugh about that.

But one thing was unmistakable. Jude knew a lot of pretty girls. The same one kept jumping out at Emmy. It was the poet from the other night. Always dressed in black, she had a smile that spoke directly to the most insecure part of Emmy's mind. *Back off, girl. He's taken.*

There they were at the lake. He had his arm around her. There again at the gelato shop, where she fed him a spoon of ice cream while he made a goofy face. Emmy couldn't see them acting that way unless there was something more between them than friendship. Her heart sank. Jude had said nothing about being in love.

Then again, it wasn't exactly the kind of thing people walked around saying in their coffee shop jobs. Did they? Emmy remembered the way they whispered together at the poetry night. She thought about the pride in his voice when he introduced her. Why wasn't there a sure sign? Some way of knowing. Emmy wished that everyone who had someone special was forced to wear a button or scarf, something to mark themselves as taken.

She'd been such a fool for thinking he could possibly want to hug her.

Then the horror of it struck her. Jude was taken, but she could not change how she felt. She was the creepy online stalker, who sat at home eating cookies, making up a life of dating Jude. *Pathetic*, she thought, as she turned off her phone. Her eyes were blurry and they hurt.

For several nights, Emmy did nothing but stare at the photos of Jude and try to dig up more. She began saving them so she wouldn't have to scroll through the images of Jude's friends and their beautiful lives. No matter how hard she tried not to look, she had to look.

Emmy hadn't updated her own accounts in ages. There they were, the same angled selfies staring into empty cyberspace. Her lips were always slightly pursed, her cheeks sucked in, like she learned from the YouTube tutorials. There were barely any likes.

Emmy woke up to the darkness of the closet. There was no way to tell if she had slept until eleven or if it was still six in the morning. She reached for her phone, but it wasn't there. She felt around. Nothing.

When she opened the door, it was light out. The clock on the wall confirmed that it was 10:30. Her aunt and uncle were already at work, but it was Tuesday so Paige might be downstairs. Emmy went to the bathroom to splash water on her face. She pulled on her hoodie and shuffled her way downstairs.

"Morning, stalker," Paige said as she entered the kitchen.

"What?"

"Emmy, you psycho," Paige said, laughing. She held Emmy's phone in her hand. She thumbed her way through a series of Jude pictures.

"How did you do that? It's password protected."

"Your fingerprint." She gave a smug smile.

"You snuck into my room and held my finger to the phone while I was sleeping? And you're calling *me* a psycho?"

"I needed your mom's number." She made it sound like it was the most natural thing in the world.

"There are easier ways, more legal ways. Don't you guys have her number stored in your home phone?"

"Um . . . bigger issue . . . why are you stalking Jude?"

"I'm not."

"Right. More than a dozen photos in your private album is definitely stalking. You weren't even there when these pics were taken. Half of them are from years ago."

Emmy knew it had been wrong to save photos off other peoples' accounts. But it was her dirty little secret. She never thought anyone would find out. She'd even made sure to hide her browsing history.

Looking at the floor, she turned on her heels and went upstairs. Nothing she could say would save her. What Paige said was true. Emmy was a pervert with an obsession that wouldn't go away no matter how hard she tried. She was a Peeping Tom sicko, confused and destined to always be alone. There was nothing to do but go back to bed and tear open her emergency stash of chocolate chip cookies.

Tears flowed and snot ran out her nose. She sat cross-legged and crunched on the dry cookies. They didn't even taste good. There was nothing good about any of this, about her life. It was just awful. What a loser she was.

Paige shouldn't have spied on her like that. But Paige was that kind of person. She ignored boundaries. That was what popular people did. They rammed themselves at you even when you told them not to. Paige had always been like that. Trying to change her would be like trying to tell a snake not to eat a baby bird. It was going against nature.

By the time the tray of cookies was almost empty, there was a knock at the door.

"Go away."

"Emmy . . . don't be upset." It was Paige's voice.

"Leave me alone."

More knocking. "I warned you to stay away from Jude."

"We're not talking about this, Paige. It's not your business. Just forget it."

The problem with closet doors is they don't lock. Paige opened the door. There was Emmy, perfectly framed in her dark cave like some kind of troll, stuffing her face with the final crumbs of a bag of cookies. She was sitting in a filthy pile of laundry, books, and random food wrappers. Emmy knew she was the image of someone who would never be kissed or get married or have one of those cute pictures with someone feeding her ice cream.

"Get lost before I throw this at you," Emmy said, reaching for a textbook.

"Fine. You deserve what you get. You two are probably meant for each other in some twisted way." Paige slammed the closet door and stalked away.

At least Paige backed off. There was that to be grateful for. Now the biggest fear Emmy had was what Paige would do with the information. Would she tell Jude? And if she did, would that confirm to Jude that he was being harassed by a pathetic loser? He'd probably forgotten all about her by now, but if Paige reminded him . . .

She had to get out. She had to deal with this horror show. What could she do now that her inner life was made public?

Emmy went downstairs, where she found her phone on the empty breakfast table. It looked abandoned, like her.

She thought about what she would say to Jude if she could. She'd tell him he was special. She'd tell him that having the pictures of him made her feel closer to him, that she hoped it wasn't weird. And in her fantasy he'd tell her that there was nothing weird about it. He'd tell her that when those pictures were taken, he had imagined his soulmate was out there somewhere. That he meant those images for someone just waiting to be a part of his life. And now here she was and it was all okay. Every step she had taken to get closer to him was fine.

Emmy felt that Jude was kind of with her everywhere she went, even in the closet. But she also knew she wouldn't actually see him if she sat at home like this.

13 Glamazon

AFTER A SHOWER and a very brief attempt at homework, Emmy got out the spare bike and helmet. This time she went in the other direction. She zigzagged through tree-lined streets. She watched the brown and orange leaves rain down on cars and sidewalks. Being in her dad's hometown made her feel closer to him. It was almost as if the city itself remembered him and could tell her more about him.

She thought about what his writing showed her. He had dealt with raw feelings too. She took comfort in that. People like Paige would never understand. *Maybe that's what bothers Paige*, Emmy thought. Maybe Paige knew that she would never be able to feel in the way that Emmy could. Maybe that's what made her mean. She was secretly jealous. And if Paige ever felt about anyone the way Emmy felt about Jude, she probably wouldn't have the courage to follow her feelings.

Emmy rode across the Granville Bridge. As she rode along Granville, she saw another side of the city. People huddled in doorways under blankets and cardboard. There was an older man wearing headphones and dancing on the street corner as though it was the middle of a dance floor. He was dressed in something out of a Michael Jackson video, all sequined and glittery. It almost hid how grubby and dirty he was. He was totally in his own world.

Emmy didn't want to stare. But from a safe distance across the street, she took in the sight of him for a long time. She saw how people walked by him, pretending they didn't see him. They totally ignored him. But he was spectacular. What were they afraid of?

For the first time, it seemed to Emmy that the whole world was afraid. The whole world, except the dancing man and maybe Jude. Emmy was afraid. What would Jude think of her if she told him everything that was in her heart? How could she show him that she thought of him as perfect?

She thought about the way girls at school had talked about this or that celebrity being so hot. Emmy had always felt alone in those conversations. She couldn't see what everyone else saw. She didn't care about what they saw in those guys. Now she knew that what made a person attractive was only partly physical. Jude was so insanely handsome to her. Yet, what drew her to him was something much, much deeper than looks alone.

Emmy clutched her phone in her hand. She had Jude's number, but only because Paige had texted them both at the same time. He hadn't given it to her. It would be stalkery to text him. He would laugh at her. He would tell her she was too young — and probably too fat — for someone like him.

She tucked her phone back in her pocket. *Would he? Could he really think that?* She knew he'd never say something like that to her. He was kind and thoughtful. Her mind filled with the look on his face that day at the park. She longed to stare into his eyes, to see the kindness deep within him. She loved the way his face tilted slightly to one side as he focused on her. She loved the way he laughed at her dorky jokes.

It would all end horribly, that was a sure thing. But she thumbed out the words.

"Hey you. What are you up to right now? Want to hang out? By the way, this is Emmy."

Before she could back out, she hit send. Then she hunched over as her insides threatened to tear her apart. Sweat poured from her forehead. What a mess. What had she done? Why was she so hopeful? So transparent? Ugh, there was nothing worse than being a pathetic girl.

The phone was back in her pocket, and her face was in her hands when she felt her phone vibrate. This was it. Expecting a text of "hahaha in yr dreams," she waited for her thumbprint to unlock the phone. Her heart pounded.

"Sure. Where?"

Emmy gasped. A yes had seemed so unlikely she couldn't believe the words on the screen.

Suddenly she panicked. She wasn't dressed to hang out. She needed deodorant and perfume and better makeup. What had she been thinking? Now it was too late. She couldn't just say she was kidding or that she texted him by accident. Or could she? People in Vancouver bailed all the time, she remembered. It was tempting.

"I'm downtown. Where are you?" she wrote.

Oh God, oh God. This was the stupidest idea. If it went bad, it'd be a disaster. If it went well, it'd be even worse. She wasn't ready for, well, anything. She didn't know the first thing about love or crushes or trans guys or guys. Nothing.

They agreed to meet at the Templeton for milkshakes. Although she had never been there, it sounded frighteningly date-like. Totally freakin' date-like. And while Emmy had given a blowjob to Ty Biggs, she had never been on that sweeter side of the couple equation. A date. Courtship. Dating. She didn't know what to do. All she knew was she had thirty minutes to get herself from where she was, near Pacific Centre, to where he would be, just a few blocks up.

She had a stroke of inspiration, and hit the MAC Cosmetics counter at The Bay. A guy in a black corset with turquoise eyeshadow approached her and asked if he could help.

"I'm actually meeting someone in a bit. I don't have any money to buy anything. You totally don't have to help, but I kind of hope you'll take pity on me. It's my first date."

"Oh, honey. Say no more. Sit down."

Emmy sat in front of a mirror and looked at herself. He explained the Adele look to her, showing her how to create the contour she wanted. Her sheer terror was obvious. No amount of putty or colour or texture could change that. But the guy came back with some stuff anyway. Emmy closed her eyes and focused on breathing as he touched her eyelids gently with his soft brush. She felt him sponge something cool onto her flushed cheeks and wipe the sweat from her brow with a delicate puff. He asked her to press her lips together and she did. When she opened her eyes, she no longer saw the pathetic creature who always looked back at her. She didn't look like Adele. She looked like herself, only better.

"Oh, my God. You're like my fairy godmother."

"You got that right," he said. He passed her samples of the various products he'd used on her.

As Emmy walked her bike up Granville, careful not to break a sweat, the autumn sun shone down on her. She thought of RuPaul and strutted like a runway model.

14 Born Naked

JUDE WAS ALREADY SEATED at a booth when Emmy walked into the retro diner. He waved.

"You look pretty today," he said when she sat down.

"I do?"

"Yeah. You did something different."

"No," she said, immediately shy. She looked at her lap. "Maybe it's because I biked." She wished she had hugged the guy in the corset. She would hug him when she went back to buy everything.

"What do you want to eat? They have great milkshakes and burgers here."

"I'm not hungry," she said. "I'll just have water. Maybe a milkshake."

"Come on. My treat. Eat something."

He hadn't mentioned eating in the text. There was no way she could eat a burger in front of Jude. It would be like being back on the stage with all those eyes on her. The skinny waitress would look at her, probably thinking she'd order a lot. And then Emmy would feel like she was in some sort of pie-eating contest in front of a crowd. That was so not going to happen with Jude right across from her.

"Just a milkshake, that's all."

"Suit yourself. I'm getting a burger. You can eat my fries if you want."

Did he think she couldn't go without? The skinny waitress with the shaved head came over and they ordered.

Being around Jude, Emmy understood why they called it butterflies. She was an anxious ball of nerves and there was fluttering deep inside her. She was so focussed on keeping the conversation going that she agreed with things Jude said without even hearing them. She was caught in her own head. It was a little like that time she was with Ty in Winnipeg, but this was worse. Ty had been quiet and had his own idea of how he wanted the night to go. She didn't get the sense that Jude wanted a blowjob or anything like that. And her mind raced. Why was he here with her? What could he possibly see in her? What *did* he want?

But she couldn't ask those questions. Instead she giggled and slurped down her mint-chocolate milkshake. She tried to pay attention to his words, even though his eyes held her mesmerized. When he looked at her she got the sense that he could see her entire past and read all her thoughts. There was nowhere to hide from Jude's gaze. It was dangerous to feel so understood and so afraid of it.

Jude was telling her about his latest busking adventure. He was describing a zany old lady when his phone buzzed on the smooth diner table. Jude grabbed it before Emmy could see who was calling.

"Sorry," he mouthed to her. He clutched the phone, and within seconds his face got all serious.

"You're kidding," he said, staring at Emmy like he was in shock. "That's so messed up . . . You're sure? . . . That's seriously messed."

When he hung up, he looked at Emmy like she was an alien, like he wanted nothing to do with her "I have to go."

"Now?"

"Right now," he said abruptly. "Finish this, okay?" He pushed the burger and fries toward her. It all but confirmed Emmy's worst nightmare — he did think she was unable to go without.

Jude got up and put on his jacket. He fished out some cash from his pocket and slapped it on the counter. Then he hurried out of the diner.

The "date" was over before Emmy knew what happened. She was alone. Was the call from Paige? Or had he simply decided that she was too fat and gross, and pretended there was some sort of emergency?

Emmy wanted to finish the milkshake, but couldn't. She had always protected herself better than this. Her world had never crumbled so completely.

"You want a box for that?" the server asked, pointing at Jude's half-eaten meal.

"No, thanks." Emmy didn't think she could ever eat again.

She spent about ten minutes stirring her melted shake and trying to drink another sip to prove she wasn't ungrateful. Then she got up and left.

Guys are shit, she thought. *All guys. Just shit.* There was no point to any of the heartache they had caused her up to now. And even Jude just picked up and left. It didn't matter if it was based on some hearsay gossip from Paige or some shallow observation of her body, which she had never hidden from him. He knew how she looked going into this thing.

She stomped her way back to her bike and plunked her helmet on her head. She made for home, which wasn't home. Halfway across the Cambie Bridge, her bike chain got stuck. The bike nearly threw her. Then she nearly threw it over the side of the bridge. She was done. Just done. How could she explain to her thin cousin that her fat ass had ruined so much?

As she walked the broken bike, she thought about home. Well, Winnipeg. It was where her mom lived, but it wasn't home. There was no home for her. She was only seventeen, but she had nothing in the world to call home. For the first time, she realized that the folks on the street were the most honest people of all. The dancer on the corner who bopped away in his own private world was quite possibly the realest guy she'd ever seen. Emmy hadn't even considered that maybe he might have wanted Jude's half-eaten burger. In the future, the only right answer to the question of taking leftovers would be yes, even if she wouldn't eat them. People outside might. Too late now. One more reason to kick herself.

Emmy huffed her way up over the bridge, walking up, up, and over to where her aunt and uncle lived. By the time she got there, she was drenched in sweat.

She dropped the bike in the garage. She raced up the stairs and into the shower. Her whole look was all gross and faded. It was time to wash it off and be totally naked. No more appearances.

Clean and towel-dried, she got into her pink fleece pants. *Guys suck. Screw them all,* she thought. She went to the fridge, filled a bowl with some bean salad and ate it quickly. She put her empty bowl in the dishwasher and sat down at the table. Time to spread the books out and get to work once and for all. It had been weeks and she hadn't completed a single unit. At this rate, she'd never graduate.

15 A Little Bit of Love

EMMY WAS DOING A MATH PROBLEM when her phone vibrated.

Now what?

It was a text from Jude.

"Sorry I left so quickly. Was upset. Did you finish the burger?"

He wanted her to give him something to chuckle at, didn't he? He could amuse himself with the image of an overweight girl sticking around to clean up his plate. Jerk.

"No. Wasn't hungry."

She could almost feel the anger bursting through her fingertips.

"Where are you?"

She rolled her eyes.

"Home. Where else?"

"Want to meet up again?"

Yeah, right. So he could make fun of her? Lead her on?

"Why?"

Then her phone rang. It was Jude. She almost didn't pick up.

But she couldn't help herself. "Yeah?" She surprised herself with her attitude.

"Are you mad at me?" he asked.

"Well . . ."

"I got pretty much the worst news I could get. I didn't know how to deal with it. But I'm calling now, aren't I?"

"Are *you* mad at *me*? You left without any explanation. What did I ever do to you?"

Besides stalk him, she thought. But since when was that a crime? If he didn't want people to look at pictures of him online, he shouldn't have posted them.

He ignored her question. "Emmy, that call I got was Clarisse telling me about a letter from the government. I got rejected for top surgery. If I want to get it, I have to come up with thousands of dollars on my own. I have nobody and nothing. I was counting on that funding. Now I don't know what to do. So, yeah, I wasn't exactly thinking about you when I left. But like I said, I'm sorry."

"Oh, Jude." At once, Emmy felt bad for assuming it was all about her.

"I get so tired sometimes. I work away at the coffee shop and a couple of weeks will go by. I save up some tip money and have some decent poets and musicians come through. And life is sort of okay, you know? But then it just kicks you right in the balls. Balls you don't have. Balls you'll never have. Because life is unfair."

"I'm sorry," Emmy whispered. She thought she heard crying, but she didn't want to ask.

"I haven't eaten since I saw you. I went home to see the letter. Not that there was any point to that. And now my blood sugar is so low I think I'm going to faint."

"Don't faint. I'll come. Where are you?"

He told her the intersection. It wasn't that far away.

When Emmy got there, Jude was already sitting at the back of the dark falafel place. There were two plates in front of him.

"I ordered for you. Hope that's okay."

"It's fine," Emmy said. But it was much more than that. No one ever ordered for her, especially not a guy, especially not Jude. She tried not to read too much into it. But wasn't that something boyfriends did? She squashed the silly thought and focused on Jude. "So what are you going to do?"

"Keep working, I guess. Get a higher paying job. Join a union. I don't know."

"But what about your music and busking and That Hashtag?"

"This is my body." He gave her a look, daring her to get it.

"And performing is your soul."

Emmy saw the surprise there before he wiped his eyes with the back of his wrist. He shook his head vigorously to get rid of the tears. "I don't know what I would do if it wasn't for Clarisse," Jude said. "I was only supposed to stay with Clarisse until the funding came through. Today she said I could stay longer, save up some money. But it's not fair to her. I feel like I'm in her way."

Suddenly Emmy didn't know why he'd brought her here or put a shawarma in front of her. None of it made sense if he already had a hot poet girlfriend. She had read an article about why men cheat with plain women. It happened when they felt like the girlfriend they chose is too far out of their league. Maybe that was what was going on.

No matter. Emmy had been selected as the shoulder to cry on. She would live up to that and prove herself worthy of being able to hold his pain. She was determined. She listened with total concentration.

But as she tried to focus on what he said about the surgery and the injustice, she couldn't shake one question. She had to know. "So is Clarisse your girlfriend or what?"

"No, no. I mean I love her and I live with her. But she's not my girlfriend."

That was just too weird. "So you mean you've broken up?"

"No, we never dated."

"But you love her?" Emmy felt like a reporter with all her questions. But she didn't want to let this go much further if she was just going to be made a fool of.

"Yeah, but not like that. She's more like my older sister."

Pretty for an older sister, Emmy quipped to herself. "Okay . . ."

"Haven't you ever had that? Someone who feels like family even though there's no blood connection?"

She shrugged.

LOVE IS LOVE

"Well, I've leaned on Clarisse ever since my family disowned me."

"They did?"

"Pretty much. I mean, I'm 'welcome back any time.'" He put the words in air quotes. "But it's not really true. Judy is welcome back. Me, not so much. Clarisse accepts me. And I accept her. That's what family really is."

"I get that," Emmy said, thinking about the distance between the members of her own family. But she couldn't tell Jude any of it. Not yet. She didn't want to scare him.

"Clarisse lets me live with her even though she's got so much bullshit to deal with. Like paying for her own hormones and surgeries. She really should boot me out and get a roommate who can pay her what the place is worth, but instead she says us trans-folks gotta stick together."

"Wow."

"So I don't know. I guess the best thing I can do is try to make a lot of money really quickly. Like maybe become a criminal or something." He smiled and for a moment Emmy saw his goofiness emerge.

"You don't mean that."

"Of course I don't. Couldn't you see it? I'd be the worst criminal ever. For one thing, you have to be able to go unnoticed. I can't even buy a damn pack of gum without people looking at me and trying to figure me out."

Emmy laughed. It was true that there were always people looking at Jude, even now. People were busy eating their falafels, sure. But they were also staring at the two of them. They were staring mostly at Jude.

When they had finished eating, Jude told Emmy he needed to go. Clarisse was off work and wanted to hang out. Emmy didn't hate Clarisse any more. Instead, she kind of loved her.

16 Looking Good, Feeling Gorgeous

THE FOLLOWING MORNING, instead of doing her homework, Emmy put on a retro green dress. Then she went to Paige's dresser and did her eyeshadow in perfect Adele style. She even used light sparkly highlight around the inner corners of her eyes. She contoured her cheekbones and everything.

Today was not a day for biking. She had too much invested. It had taken an hour to get the makeup just right and her dress was too stiff to bike in. Because she could, because her textbooks would wait for another day, she had put her hair in rollers. Now she let down long, loose curls. It was about as good as she was capable of looking. All there was to do was pop Adele into her earbuds and stroll down the street to Jude's coffee shop. She had to hear how he was doing. He might as well see her looking like a million bucks. Walking down Main Street, she caught glimpses of herself in shop windows and the glass confirmed the truth. She was not a hideous beast.

Emmy sauntered through the door and glanced around. She made eye contact with the people who looked up to see who was coming in. She was making an entrance, the way Paige did, the way the two musician-poets did, the way Adele did. The only unusual part was that it was her. Otherwise there was nothing weird about people looking. People always looked at people who were strange or beautiful.

Jude noticed her right away. He waved from behind the counter. She felt the bounce of her hair with each step as she walked toward him.

"What'll it be, miss?" Jude asked in a mock-British accent.

"A toasted coconut caramel latte, please. Large." Why not? A bold drink for a bold day.

Behind her, Emmy heard the sound of a girl laughing. *It was probably nothing*, Emmy thought. *Just a shared joke or something.* There were two girls behind her. They were Paige's age, maybe. They looked like they worked in a tanning salon, with their bleached hair and tight-fitting yoga pants. Emmy moved aside to let them order.

"I'll have an Americano," one said. "With a bit of steamed skim."

"Seriously?" her friend said to her. "Why don't you get yourself a fat-girl drink with whip? You've been so good lately."

They cracked up. Emmy went red.

"Um, excuse me?" Jude asked the one who had made the joke.

"Never mind," she said.

"Oh, I'll mind," Jude said. There was anger in his

voice. Emmy hadn't heard that before. "Because let me tell you something." He gestured at Emmy. "She is a hell of a lot more beautiful than either of you ever could be. Do you know why? Because she is kind and you two are horrible."

"Whoa, whoa, whoa. That's uncalled for," one of the girls said. "I want to talk to the manager."

"Tough shit. The manager is not here right now. And I refuse to serve fat-phobic mean girls."

The girls glared at Jude, trying to knock him down with their hateful stares.

Jude held his ground. "You heard me. You can go."

They turned and bolted. Jude looked satisfied with himself. Emmy turned the colour of a lobster.

Jude went over to the espresso machine and began frothing milk.

"You know, on second thought, maybe I'll have an Americano," Emmy said meekly.

"No way. Not because of them. Don't give them that," Jude answered.

Emmy didn't know what to say. She found herself

studying the counter instead. There were some wet spots and a dirty rag on the corner.

"You didn't have to defend me, you know," she finally managed in a low voice. She wanted to tell him that if they ever had another encounter like that, she'd rather he just ignore it. The attention was worse than the insult.

"I couldn't *not* say anything."

Emmy couldn't imagine getting into a fight with strangers — pretty strangers — just because they said something unkind. That was their right as pretty girls, wasn't it?

Jude put the coconut caramel latte in front of Emmy. The whipped cream made her feel ashamed. She could tell Jude wanted her to take pleasure in it. But she felt like she'd taken too much pleasure in calorie-rich drinks. She wore the burden of it on her frame. *This dress would look so much better,* she thought, *if I could just get down to the size I was when I sucked in in front of the mirror.* And the latte was not going to help. It was her enemy. She didn't want to touch it. But Jude had made it. It sat there, on the counter, tormenting her.

She took the drink to her table and plunked it down. She put down her coat and textbooks, too. She watched the whipped cream melt and sink into the sweet coffee below. Then she went to the washroom. In the privacy of the overly fragrant stall, she burst into tears. She could never cry like this out there. It was impossible.

She had no idea how much time passed as she cried. There was a knock at the door.

"You okay in there?" It was Jude.

"I'm fine," she sniffled.

"Get out here," he commanded.

"In a minute."

"Now."

She said nothing, but began wiping her face with toilet paper. Dusty white bits stuck to the sides of her cheekbones. Her makeup was ruined. She looked like a sewer rat. A fat sewer rat.

"I have a key," Jude said. "I'll give you thirty more seconds."

But he didn't. He busted open the door and she stood there, exposed. It was exactly what she did not want.

"Come here," he said. He grabbed her by the arms at first, then held her to him. "I'm not a hugger. But you need a hug, so I'm making an exception."

"Thank you," she whispered.

"You're beautiful, you know. Don't let horrible people project their stupid shit on you."

She didn't know what he meant. So she lingered on the one word she had never heard anyone say to her before, not the way Jude said it. *Beautiful.*

No, she wasn't. She knew that. The word "beautiful" described girls in ads and on TV. It referred to girls like the two who had just left. It was girls who were thin enough to wear yoga gear in public. Emmy knew that at best she had charm and a good personality. Even that was debatable. But she wasn't beautiful. She was sure of that.

Still, she clung to Jude in the privacy of the washroom. She let him hold her when she needed holding and breathed in the orangey scent of his subtle cologne. It was something she could live on for the days, weeks and months to come. Emmy ran her hands up Jude's back, closing the space between them, sealing it with their body heat. She felt the slight bulge of his binding. So strange to think there were breasts under there. They seemed out of place. Emmy thought that she understood him more because of it. She too had things that were out of place and not what she wanted. Since he was beautiful, maybe she could be too.

17 Hiding My Love

IN THE KITCHEN BACK AT THE HOUSE, Emmy figured that dinnertime in Winnipeg was probably a good time to catch her mom. It had been a while since their last talk. Emmy held out hope that they might have a better conversation this time. Maybe she'd get the sense that she was missed. She pressed the green button on her phone to connect.

On the screen, there was a flash of the ceiling and the casserole on the dinner table. It felt like ages since Emmy had eaten a good solid prairie casserole with hashbrowns and sour cream and cheddar cheese. Vancouver was all about kale and quinoa. She hadn't been hungry before, but she sure was now.

"Emmy," her mom said, "I'm taking you into the other room."

Ron protested. "Ach. Ruth, come on. You're the one that insisted we sit down as a family."

"I'll only be a couple of minutes."

"Well, I'm gonna watch the game then."

"Suit yourself," her mother huffed. Emmy almost got dizzy as her mom walked through the hallway into the bedroom. She heard the door close and watched her mom's face get serious.

"So what's this about you having a transgender boyfriend?"

"What?"

"Paige told Linda. There's no point in hiding it. What the hell are you up to out there? Why aren't you doing the one thing you're supposed to be doing? Don't you want to graduate?"

"It's fine. I'm on top of it. Unit one is pretty much all done."

"It's almost November. Shouldn't you be further along?"

"It's fine, Mom. Really."

"I don't like the sound of this transgender boyfriend thing. And I hear he keeps a filthy woman in tow."

"First of all, Jude is not my boyfriend and he doesn't keep Clarisse *in tow*. Secondly, I don't like the way you say transgender like it's a bad thing."

"Well, it isn't a plus, that's for sure."

"You don't even know anyone trans. What do you know about it?"

"Enough to know that this is a complication that you don't need in your life. Not with everything you've been through and everything you've come from."

"What the hell is that supposed to mean?"

Her mom sighed. "Why do girls always fall for some version of their dad?"

"Dad wasn't trans."

"No, that was one thing he didn't get to in his lifetime. And I thank God for that."

Emmy scoffed. "Why are you bringing Dad into this?"

"Because, Emmy, I want better for you than you want for yourself. I want you to find someone normal who will love you in a normal way. Don't settle for this Jude character. It's too much weirdness for you. The last thing you need is to be the normal one in a relationship."

"That's a horrible thing to say."

"Well, it needs saying. I'll tell you one thing. You don't have to make life harder on yourself than it already is."

Emmy let out a big sigh. There was no way she'd convince her mom Jude's mere existence meant the world was a better place. Her mom would never see that it took so much bravery to be Jude. Emmy didn't want to hear any more about what her mom thought about Jude or trans people or anything. Never had the woman been so wrong . . . except maybe when she talked about Emmy's dad.

"Are you in love with Ron?" Emmy interrupted, taking charge of the conversation.

"I love him. Sure."

"But are you *in love* with him?"

"Ron is a good man, a decent man. Don't turn this around on me. You think you're so clever. But I'm on your side here."

"I guess that's all I needed to hear."

"That I'm on your side?"

"No, the part about Ron."

"Emmy." Her mom scowled.

Emmy was sick of holding back. "You don't know what I'm feeling, okay? You could never understand it. *I* don't even understand it. What Jude makes me feel when we're together, it's unlike anything."

"Has he been improper with you?"

"Mom, no. Ew. Who talks like that? He doesn't even know I like him. I mean he knows I think he's cool. But everyone thinks he's cool."

"Hippie town." Her mom rolled her eyes.

"He'd never go for me anyway. Not in a million years."

"Why do you always put yourself down like that? I mean, it's good, I guess. Don't encourage him."

"Thanks for the excellent life advice, Mom. Don't follow your heart or feel things. Just be normal and boring."

"There's a reason you think normal is boring, Emmy, and it isn't healthy. How are you doing with your meds, by the way?"

She *would* bring that up. "Fine. Regular. Nothing new."

"I have to get back to dinner." Her mom was already moving through the hallway.

"I should go, too."

They hung up. Emmy sat down and took in the scene. There was her mom and this strange man they'd known for less than two years and his kid. They all seemed really happy with each other. It wasn't disgusting just because it seemed like one of those old-timey Norman Rockwell paintings. Something else about it bothered Emmy. Now she finally got it. It was the fact that her dad had been erased.

Then it really hit her. Her mom was so normal. Normal the way her dad had never been. Normal the way Emmy wasn't. And all her mom wanted was for her family to be normal.

All Emmy wanted to do was see Jude. She wanted to tell him about her dad. Thinking about it consumed her. But she couldn't share everything with him. She didn't have the nerve. Her mom, as much as it pained Emmy to admit, was right. Emmy was not a healthy person. Her dad was not a healthy guy, either. She barely remembered ever seeing him sober. But somehow she felt that Jude might understand. For the first time in her life, it felt like there was someone who wanted to know about her and who just might actually get her. And that thought was delicious. Maybe it wasn't normal, but it meant everything.

Her dad had spent his whole life putting stuff into himself to ease the pain of existing. And she did that too. How many hours could she go without eating? Not the 'normal' amount between meals, that was for sure. And why? Food made her happy. She couldn't stop thinking about it. She hated being addicted to food, hated it with all her might. But could she change? No. There was no way. She had been like this for as long as she could remember.

And now Jude was like those President's Choice cookies, like her morning cereal, like the Burger King Whopper. She just had to have him. She would never, ever be in a normal relationship. Not if normal was being like her mom and Ron. But Emmy realized she wanted no part in that. You pick someone that you kind of like. Sure they have a ton of irritating qualities, but you're willing to put up with them because it's better than facing a life of being alone. Then you shack up and get on each other's nerves. You argue about stupid stuff and feel resentful most of the time. Somehow that's supposed to be love? That's normal? The whole picture was a mess.

18 Dumb

EMMY'S PHONE VIBRATED. It was Jude.

"You ok?"

So simple. Two words. They showed he cared. She thumbed out a paragraph in response.

"I just got off the phone with my mom. She clearly thinks I'm nuts and I think I am, too. I want to tell you all the stuff that is wrong with me. But I'm afraid of scaring you away because you're the best thing that has ever happened to me."

She deleted it. Too much.

She tried again.

"Thank you for asking. Sometimes I think you're the only one who cares. You matter so much to me. Maybe that's a weird thing to say."

She deleted that too.

Finally she wrote, "I'm okay."

Okay meant okay. She wasn't lying. She didn't say she was good or healthy or happy or normal. She said she was okay, as in breathing, living, existing.

Her mom was right about one thing. It wasn't fair to inflict herself on Jude. Jude had enough troubles without also having a crazy girlfriend, if her being his girlfriend was even possible. If by some small chance he actually was able to like her back and be attracted to her and they were a *thing*, then that would be unfair and horrible. But her mom had it wrong. Of the two of them, Emmy and Jude, it was Jude who was the mentally healthier one. He didn't have addictions and obsessions. He wasn't on mood stabilisers. He didn't get pulled out of classes to see the school psychologist all the freakin' time. The more she thought about it, the more Emmy felt guilty about presenting herself as someone who had it even remotely together.

It was time to cut herself off. She didn't deserve Jude and he most definitely did not deserve to have a crazy person glom onto him. He had hugged her. He had sent her a text to show he cared. He was a good person. She couldn't do this to him. She couldn't consume him. Better to live and die alone. Better to face the demons alone. She listened to Kurt Cobain for an hour, lying on a mattress on the floor of a dark closet in a city that was way too slick. Emmy finally texted Jude.

"I don't know what we're doing. I don't think I can see you anymore."

She stared at the words. Tears welled in her eyes as she sat cross-legged, cradling her phone. She didn't deserve his arms around her. She wasn't capable of loving him or having him love her. She thought about RuPaul saying, "if you don't love yourself how in the hell you gonna love somebody else?" She had a long way to go before she could do either.

Send.

She put her face in her palms and sobbed. It was cruel to send words like that without knowing where he was or what he was doing. But she couldn't face him.

She kept looking at her phone to see if he was writing something. He wasn't. She ate some chocolate chip cookies and some Old Dutch regular chips, adding to the mountain of shame building up in the corner of the closet. She would have to remember to sneak out the garbage.

Her dad's notebook called to her and she read more about his demons. How he wrote so much about getting fucked up was a mystery.

Hours passed. Still nothing. She had been ghosted.

And then it hit her. She knew where she belonged. It called to her like chocolate chip cookies. She got dressed, but didn't bother brushing her teeth or putting on makeup. She zipped up her hoodie and hid in the darkness of the hood. It was raining out and she didn't feel like biking.

She walked to the liquor store at Kingsgate Mall. At first, she stood outside, looking in, wondering if she really had it in her. She had never stolen anything before.

Once she was inside, she spotted the security guard near the back. So she walked over to the vodka aisle, stuffed a small flat bottle into the front pocket of her hoodie and bolted for the door. Her heart was pounding. But once she was outside, she thought it was the easiest thing she'd ever done.

She sat down on a bench across the street to collect her thoughts. It had been too easy. It was wrong. She had to go back.

Emmy approached a man heading into the Liquor Store. "Can you put this on the counter for me?" She passed him a ten-dollar bill.

He eyed her suspiciously. "I'm not buying booze for you."

"I'm not asking you to."

"Do it yourself, then."

"Just give it to the cashier," Emmy huffed. "Plunk it down on the counter. That's all I'm asking."

Maybe she was destined to be an alcoholic. But she was no thief.

If reading her dad's notebooks and watching hours of Kurt Cobain interviews had taught her anything, it was that getting drunk was no big deal. Her aunt and uncle wouldn't think so, so she'd have to keep it hidden. But she knew how. She sat in the park all by herself and took several sips straight from the bottle. It stung her throat. But that didn't matter. She was thinking about her dad's notebooks and love and pain.

She texted Paige, trying to sound sassy.

"Whatcha doin'?"

"With friends. ;-)"

"Can I join?"

"If you want."

She wobbled her way across the street to Sushi Yama where Paige was eating with her friends. They all were deep into one of Paige's stories. New people this time, but they were still hanging on her every word.

"I couldn't believe it," Paige continued. She didn't even notice Emmy behind her. "He said that he just didn't think I was smart enough."

"Were those his exact words?" one girl wanted to know.

"His exact words, right after we made out were, 'you are really hot, but I can't risk my career for this. I don't think the intellectual link is there.'"

The whole table of young women exploded in outrage.

"I can't believe he made out with you."

"You should really take that to the dean."

As Paige looked around, taking in the support, she noticed Emmy. "Oh, hey," she said. "Everyone, this is my cousin."

Noticing that Paige left her unnamed, irrelevant, she added, "I'm Emmy."

"We were just talking about how I was sexually harassed by my TA," said Paige as Emmy sat down.

"The guy you've been throwing yourself at?" Emmy asked. It was the liquid courage talking.

Everyone stared at her.

Paige scoffed. "What the hell is wrong with you?"

Emmy smirked.

"Wait a second. Are you drunk?"

Emmy shrugged.

"You are, aren't you?" Paige examined Emmy's face. "You're so busted. How much have you had?"

"It doesn't matter."

"I can't babysit you. And you can't go home like this." Paige told her friends she'd be back in two minutes. She took Emmy by the arm and pulled her out onto the street. To Emmy's horror, Paige dragged Emmy to Jude's coffee shop.

Emmy protested. "I can't go in there. I can't see him. You were right. It's no good."

"What the hell else am *I* supposed to do with you?" Paige asked, pulling her through the door. She plunked Emmy down at the counter in front of Jude.

Emmy clung to Paige. She felt like she was about to get tossed into the deep end of a pool. "Don't make me."

Paige ignored her and turned to Jude. "I don't know how this happened. But she's your problem now. Get her home safe."

"I'm fine," Emmy protested. *Hiccup*. Woops. They'd walked so fast.

Jude looked at Emmy with concern on his face. Then he laughed. The laughter made a point of anger spark under the boozy haze Emmy felt. *He* was the one who had ghosted *her*. It was as though her break-up text never even happened.

"Are you drunk?" Jude asked.

"I'm fine."

"I got this," Jude said to Paige.

Paige turned to leave. "Text me if you need me to drive. Otherwise, I'm working on finals."

19 Come As You Are

AS SOON AS PAIGE was out the door, Jude shook his head at Emmy.

"What am I supposed to do with you?" Jude asked, smiling.

Emmy shrugged. It was weird to see him acting normal with her. Acting like it was all fine. She'd spent the evening feeling dumped and pathetic and heartbroken.

"I've got another three hours on my shift.

Everything will look very different by then, I'm sure. So I'm just going to put this in front of you." Jude took a sandwich from the display fridge. He put it on a plate and slid it onto the counter. "Eat."

"I'm messed up, Jude," Emmy said, trying not to look at the sandwich or Jude. "I'm messed in ways I can't even begin to tell you about."

"Same here."

He turned back to his other customers. Emmy watched him in action. There was nothing like seeing him work the place, getting his customers laughing and at ease. She was amazed how well his pained heart could hide behind his charm. No one there but Emmy could see what kind of fortress Jude lived in. He had a moat around him and a drawbridge he had let down for her a few times. But he could close it up and withstand any storm, to stand alone without needing anyone or anything.

In lull moments Jude checked to see that she'd eaten a few bites. The place was hopping, the tips were piling up and Jude was in his element.

"So it's official," Emmy announced to Jude. "I can't go back to Winnipeg."

"What? Why not?"

"Because my mom's a whore."

"Your mom is a sex worker? You never told me that." He gave her a look of surprise.

"No, she's an office worker. But she's a whore."

"Emmy." Jude's face was stern. He frowned in disgust. "Don't use that word."

Emmy rolled her eyes. But she could see that Jude was serious. As serious as when he threw out the yoga girls.

"Emmy, I feel really strongly about this. If a woman exchanges sex for money, she's a sex worker. If she doesn't, and even if she does, don't call her a whore. It's sexist. Worse than that, it puts down sex workers. And not only are they people worthy of respect, they can be some of the best people in the world."

There's Jude on his soapbox again, thought Emmy. *So many opinions.*

"Sorry," she said. But even to her it didn't sound like she meant it.

Jude wouldn't let it go. "Clarisse does sex work. So when you insult your mom by using that word, you make it my business to call you on it."

"I didn't mean it like that."

"Emmy, I need you to understand. Clarisse's work pays for her hormones. And she lets me live with her so I can afford the treatment I need. I don't want to think of you, someone I was actually starting to trust, as being so insensitive." He shook his head.

Emmy couldn't take any more. It was one thing when she was the wronged one. But she couldn't face the disappointment in his eyes. And she couldn't hole up in the washroom again. Jude was stuck behind the counter for another hour. He wouldn't come after her if she left. Not now. Probably not ever. Emmy rushed out the door.

For the first time in ages, she longed for The Peg. Back there, she could use that word to describe her mom. Her friends did it all the time. It didn't mean anything. Having Jude explain it to her made her feel like a hick. It proved that she was an outsider in his life.

But now there was nowhere to go. She couldn't go back to Linda and Frank's. There was no point in calling Paige. Emmy had no friends in the world. So she went back to Dude Chilling Park and sat on a bench. There was another drunk person on another bench, but he was nearly passed out. He had his head down in his lap, grumbling about something.

There were a lot of people, even at night. And there were pathways and it wasn't really that dark. The booze had worn off, and there was more than half a bottle left. She pressed the lip of it to her mouth. The vodka burned going down her throat and gave a brief feeling of warmth. But she was cold through, the evening wind chilling her to the bone. *They say that Manitoba is cold,* Emmy thought, *but really this is far colder.*

She pulled her knees up to her chest and wrapped her coat around her. She spread her scarf up around her face. *This is it,* she thought, looking out at the moon-streaked park. This was where she could finally let it all out. She bawled.

Emmy had never felt so alone. Everyone left her. Her dad went and died. Her mom sent her away. Her so-called friends didn't even bother to stay in touch. Paige palmed her off on anyone. And now Jude. It was tiring, the way everyone kept disappearing.

Another sip. Another.

Emmy didn't know how long she had been sitting and drinking when they walked up to her.

"Got enough to share?" one of them asked. He introduced himself as Jaiden.

He looked nice enough. So did his two friends. She eyed her nearly empty bottle, shrugged, and passed it to him. He took a sip. She was surprised by the friendly the way he looked at her. Maybe like he thought she was kind of pretty.

"Why are you out here alone?" Jaiden asked.

She shrugged again. How could she even begin to explain?

"Not much for words, eh?"

Another shrug. Jaiden sat down next to her. *Why is he crashing my pity party?* Emmy wondered. She didn't want it to turn into an actual party. Not when she'd lost the closest thing she'd ever had to love. But even though they made her nervous, Emmy felt pressure to impress them. She should be nice and all that.

"What are you up to?" she asked.

"Not much. Walking around. Seeing what's up."

"Oh, yeah," Emmy said, loosening up. "Sounds better than my night."

"Something wrong?" He put his arm along the back of the bench. "You can tell me."

Talking to strangers was easier than sitting alone with no one. "I think I broke up with someone," Emmy said.

"You think? Or you did?" Jaiden asked.

Thinking about the difference made Emmy confused. The whole thing was still fuzzy in her mind. "Well, we weren't even really together. So I dunno."

"Sounds messy." He turned the corners of his mouth downward like he was sad for her. She liked the way he looked closely at her. His probing questions showed he must care.

Jaiden put his hand on her knee and nodded to his friends. As the other two closed in on them, Emmy suddenly felt that the closeness was wrong. Her body tensed. Her back became rigid and her jaw clenched.

Jaiden didn't seem to notice or care. "Well, you know what they say. The best way to get over someone is to get under someone else." He laughed at his own joke. His friends laughed along. To Emmy it sounded like hyenas cackling.

"Dude, remember sharing?" one of them said. "It looks like there's enough there to go around."

Emmy knew he wasn't talking about the vodka.

That was when it all became clear. She didn't want to let herself get hurt. Not even if she tried to call it something else, like sex or love. Not by Ty, not by this moron. Not by anyone. She knew in that moment that she loved herself. She cared about herself too much to fall into this trap again.

"I gotta go," she said, getting to her feet.

"Was it something I said?" Jaiden asked.

"Yeah, actually. I am not your low self-esteem hook-up girl, okay? I wasn't sitting around waiting for you to come along and take pity on me."

And with that she was walking away.

20 *One and Only*

EMMY RAN TO THE COFFEE SHOP. Broken as it all was, she wanted to fix things. She had to see Jude before it was too late. She could see from a block away that the lights were already out. But she could make out Jude's shadow as he locked the side door.

"I had a feeling you'd be back," he said.

"I'm sorry," Emmy said, gasping for breath. "For everything."

"You don't need to be," Jude said.

"But I am. I never want to hurt your feelings or say bad things about the people you love."

He grasped her cold hands in his and breathed hot air onto them. Their eyes met. Jude took her in his arms and held her. He told her softly that he was sorry too. He kissed the top of her head and she let her tears flow right into that safe place where his shoulder met his neck. Emmy thought about Jude's issues with touching. She marvelled at how right it felt to be in his arms.

Emmy knew that here, she could let herself feel. With Jude, she could be everything. She could be the vulnerable girl who would do anything to be liked. She could be the strong girl who could bike and run and do anything she wanted. She could be the girl whose heart broke at the thought of losing Jude forever.

"Jude," she said in a quiet voice. "I'm sorry I'm messed up. I'm sorry I don't know how to be with other people. But one thing I'm not sorry about is how I feel about you."

"Emmy," he said. "Emmy. Emmy. Emmy."

Emmy was warm everywhere. She couldn't believe this feeling was possible.

With Jude's arms around her, Emmy was both terrified and at ease. All the running she'd done in her life ended in this moment. This was it. She didn't need to escape anymore because she was where she needed to be.

It was the happiness that finally made her cry. She said, "Sometimes it feels like I don't deserve you."

"Me? That's how I feel about you. Ever since you've been here I've been wondering what I did to deserve your attention. You get me. All my life I've felt like nobody would ever get me, ever see the real me." He dried a tear from Emmy's eye.

"I see you," she said with a sniffle.

"I know you do. I feel it."

"Jude," she said. She clutched him close to her.

"I want to take you to one of my special spots. My bike's locked up around back. We can go to your place and get yours."

"It's broken."

"What do you mean it's broken?"

"The chain fell off."

"I can fix that," Jude said.

"You don't have to."

"I want to."

"I don't know if we have tools in the garage."

He smiled. "I have tools."

At the surprising image of Jude fixing her bike, Emmy had to smile back.

The booze had worn off by the time Jude finished his handiwork. Despite Emmy's doubts about his skills as a bike mechanic, it didn't take much for him to fix it. He knew exactly what he was doing.

Soon Emmy was pedaling after him across the Cambie Bridge, the night sky cool against her face. The glossy city was aglow with the sparkling lights of condos and retail shops and tall glass buildings. She could barely take it all in as they rode along the seawall.

They biked, alone together, for nearly an hour before arriving at Second Beach.

Jude stopped and locked up his bike, then hers. He took Emmy by the hand and walked her to the swing set. She sat on the cool plastic seat and put her hands on the metal chains. Jude stood behind her, holding her. She felt his warm breath on the top of her head.

She had dreamed of this moment all her life. But the reality of it made her sad. Now that she was seeing what real love was, she wasn't ready for it.

"Everything I've learned about love and romance makes me want to avoid it," Emmy said. "My mom hated my dad before he died. She was in the middle of divorcing him anyway." She had never told that truth to anyone. It was easier to let them think her dad's death was the only tragedy. It was easier to understand death than to get your head around falling out of love and fighting constantly. Emmy muffled a cry as she added, "He was drinking and driving. That's how he died."

Jude held her tight. All the times she'd thought about telling Jude about her dad, she saw herself breaking down and bawling. But she didn't. It helped that he held her and just listened.

A couple of minutes later, Jude spoke. "My parents are still together, but only because they have to be. No divorce in my family. But plenty of misery."

So he did understand. Everyone else she'd ever met seemed to believe in romance, even the ones who called themselves cynical. They weren't like her. No one was like her in that honesty about the world. Except maybe Jude.

"I never want to make you miserable," Emmy said.

"You couldn't. You make me happy."

"You know what's strange? Every romantic movie I ever watched and every romance novel I ever read, it's the girl. She's always the one who wants to be in a relationship. She can't wait. But I'm scared of it. I'm scared of hurting you. I'm scared of being a mess you have to clean up."

"Oh, Emmy."

Jude turned her around by twisting the two metal chains together. He stood in front of her and held her to his chest. Emmy put her ear against him and listened to his heartbeat. She ached to be as close to him as she could. Even the swing's chains were too much of a barrier between them. She stood up and wrapped her arms around him.

21 *If I Dream*

THERE, WHILE SHE WAS STILL tangled up in the swing, Jude kissed her. It was long and slow and Emmy felt it down to her knees. Even her hips felt looser, and she longed to lie down with him. She wanted to wrap her legs around him. She wanted to hold him in every way that she could.

For a long time, they said nothing, just held on to each other. Jude ran his hands up and down her back. Emmy was terrified that he could feel the bulges of her bra strap, how the tightness cut into her flesh. Being judged by him would break her heart.

"I used to think I was asexual," Jude whispered. "Not anymore."

Emmy smiled. "Really?"

Jude nodded.

She took him by the hand and led him to a bench that looked out over the water. There were a few people here and there, but mostly they were alone in the cool evening breeze. Cuddling with Jude, Emmy felt sheltered against the cold. Together they created a tiny bubble of space just for them.

Emmy ran her hands up his back and placed her palms on his neck. She stroked his warm skin. He seemed to soften at her touch. She liked what it did to his face, how he looked relaxed. He looked pleasured. He kissed her more. Nothing had ever felt so natural, so good.

"You're so beautiful," he told her.

She thought that he was too. But she wouldn't use that word. Handsome was probably a better word.

Good looking. Hot. She couldn't begin. And anyway, there was so much more to it than how he looked. She said nothing, preferring instead to show him.

Her hands explored. She was aware of the physical tension that she'd felt that first day, when she saw him at the coffee shop. She needed to show him how she'd wanted since then to touch him. She caressed his cheek and ran her hand down his front. Even beneath his fall sweater she could feel the binding there. She placed her hand on his heart, wanting badly to feel the beat of it through her palm. Jude tensed and sat back. Suddenly he was stiff, awkward.

"Don't." He shook his head. She knew right away that the touch felt wrong to him. Emmy withdrew her hand.

"I'm sorry."

He looked away, out over the water. The lit-up freighters cast their glow into the bay. Though the lights were warm, the ships seemed lonely out there. Emmy said nothing. Her palms sweated over the thought that she'd ruined everything. But she waited.

She hoped Jude wasn't going to get up and leave. She wanted to give him time.

"I can't be touched there," he said. "Not like that."

"I didn't mean to," Emmy said. She wished she hadn't. She wished she could take the touch back. She wanted to explain about his heartbeat, how she'd heard it earlier and wanted to feel it enter her through her palms. But it seemed like such a weird thing to say that she didn't.

"It's not you." Jude turned to her and looked into her eyes. "It's never you."

Emmy looked out at the ocean.

"I just want to be a regular guy, you know? I want to do all the stuff that regular guys do. But then I remember that I'm not, that I can't."

"I like the way you are," Emmy said quietly.

Jude kind of chuckled to himself. It was as if he couldn't believe what she was saying. He looked away. Emmy thought that maybe he was nervous. But she could wait. She would wait as long as it took.

"It scares me that you like me," he finally said.

"Because I'm some kind of horror movie monster?"

"God, no. What scares me is not being able to give you what you need. What if I get close to you and then you find out I can't give you what you really want?"

"I want *you*," Emmy said, surprising herself.

He semi-laughed again. "You say that, but you don't know. What if I can't *provide* in the way any other guy could?"

"I don't need you to . . . provide." Whatever that meant.

"I don't have . . . I can't . . . I don't even know how to say what I want to say. I'm not like other guys."

Emmy didn't need him to say it. She got it. It was about the physical side of things. Right now, Jude had breasts, like Emmy did, even though he kept them bound. He didn't have, well, typical guy equipment down there. Emmy thought about Ty and Jaiden and how unfair it was. Those guys had been born with the equipment but didn't know what to do with it. They were unworthy.

"You're the guy I want to be with." Emmy couldn't believe she'd been brave enough to tell the truth. But whatever Jude felt about her, he had to know that he was all the guy she'd ever wanted. "Oh, God. I felt so bad about having a crush on you. I never thought I'd be able to admit it to you."

"Why not?" He looked confused.

"I just . . . I figured there's no way you'd ever go for me."

"Why wouldn't I?"

"Do I really need to say it?" She put her hand on her hip. She brought his attention to her figure by slowly moving her hand toward her belly. "There's all this. And you're so much cooler than me. More outgoing. Stylish." She saw him look down at the checkered shirt he was wearing beneath his thin wool sweater. She realized he had no idea about the effect his confidence had on other people. But she went on. "And you're older. Everything. There's nothing about you that made me think you could ever be interested in me."

"Even the way I followed you around like a puppy dog?" he asked.

"Did you?"

"You didn't notice?"

"I wasn't sure. You were nice to all the other girls that came into the coffee shop, too."

"Baristas are nice," he said defensively. "We have to be. You didn't notice the way I kept staring at you? I was pretty self-conscious about that."

"I had nothing to compare it to. I thought you liked to look at people."

"God, Emmy, where do you come from?" He shook his head and laughed. "Come here."

He put his arms around her and pulled her close. He traced her hairline with his fingers and gripped her by the hair. He wasn't forceful, but he let her know exactly where he wanted her. She closed her eyes and he kissed her.

As they sat closer than Emmy thought two people

could be, the breeze rolled in off the ocean with its scent of cold and wet and distance. The strangeness of it made her think of how far she was from Winnipeg. She remembered how she'd been afraid to leave. Changing who she was, taking a leap of faith had been unthinkable then. Maybe it was her dad's west coast heart that had called to her, urged her out here to find his journals, find his city, find herself. Change was a frightening thing. Like being honest about feelings, like trying to figure out love. But now she was here. This was perfection. And if she hadn't followed her heart she wouldn't be here now.

"You know what, Jude? All my life, I've felt out of place and I just realized something."

"What's that?"

"I'm home."

Acknowledgements

First and foremost, I want to thank my editor Kat Mototsune, without whom this book would not exist. Thank you, Kat, for believing that girls like Emmy should get the guy and that guys like Jude should get to be the romantic love interest.

Many people helped to shape this project. Most notably: Elaine Yong, Cecilia Leong, Andrea Warner, Jackie Wong, Cathleen With, Karen X. Tulchinsky, Amanda Hamm, Billeh Nickerson, and Tony Correia. Thank you for letting me be my seventeen-year-old self with you, for talking Adele and RuPaul, and for reminiscing about crushes and the horror of having feelings.

I want to thank my mom for not being like Emmy's mom.

For reading early drafts and giving feedback on this manuscript, as well as providing endless moral support, I would especially like to thank Bren Robbins.